To Joanna and Stephen

With special thanks to
Cami Aston

Contents

Chapter 1

The Silver Cloud

The Silver Cloud sped downhill, following the winding path between the empty caravans. Steven was flushed with excitement, sweaty with effort, his dark eyes straining against the dusk.

The Silver Cloud was his own handiwork, his pride and joy. It was a cart, made from off-cuts of wood from a timber merchant's and four pram wheels from the tip. Steven and Lucy had built it themselves, while Dad helped and advised. Steven had painted the frame silver. With his feet on the cross bar and his hands on the rope, he could steer very accurately. He remembered its first run. He and Lucy had tossed a coin to decide who went first, and he'd won. Mum had come out of the cottage to watch and cheer, then dashed back in for her camera.

Now he hurtled downwards, gaining speed, the wind making his ears smart. As he rounded the last bend, the end of the run came into sight. The Silver Cloud didn't have any brakes, but Steven usually solved that problem by guiding her up a grassy bank. He usually landed expertly, falling off safely, laughing and gasping. But now his exit was blocked. A plump, scowling boy, wearing a shirt with Chicago Bulls on the front, sat astride a gleaming red mountain bike in front of the bank. "Look out!" Steven yelled, "Coming in to land!"

Taken by surprise, the boy scooted his bike to the side and watched, amazed, as Steven guided the cart up the home stretch, and fell off a bit more breathlessly than usual.

"Wha' d'ya think you're doing?" the boy drawled. "Ya coulda damaged my bike with that heap of garbage!"

Steven leapt to his feet, shaking bits of grass out of his spikey dark hair. Wow! The kid's American! he thought, impressed, but he shouted indignantly, "It's not a heap of garbage! And you were standing right in front of my landing stage!"

"Landing stage!" the boy mocked. "Can't your dad afford to buy you a bike? Is that why you ride around on this pile of wood and nails?"

Steven stood up straight and stiff. His arms were by his sides, but his fists were clenched. The boy spotted them. "Wanna fight, then?" he goaded. His fair hair was neatly slicked back. His cheeks were pink with anticipation.

Looking him up and down, Steven considered the boy's size and weight for a moment. He must be about twelve, the same age as Steven himself, but he was a little taller, and much heavier.

"What's the matter? You chicken?"

In one agile movement, Steven dragged the new-comer from his bike in a head-lock, and brought him crashing to the ground. The boy landed heavily, pulling Steven down with him. Puffing and grunting, the stranger swung his fists in all directions. Steven wriggled and dodged, ducked and rolled, but eventually the bigger boy landed a heavy blow on his eye. Clapping a hand to his face, Steven pulled away, gasping, stunned for a moment. Then, indignant and angry, he leapt back at the American, and they rolled, locked together, down the grassy slope that Steven used to stop the Silver Cloud.

They landed, out of breath, a tangle of arms and legs. Sitting up, Steven fingered his throbbing cheek bone. It felt like an egg. He peered over it, out of his smarting, closing eye. The two boys stared at one another, scowling. Gathering his strength, Steven bunched his fists and rained punches, hard and fast, over the heavy boy's chest, shoulders and head.

"One for my dad," he panted, thumping with all his strength. He had one knee on the boy's chest. "One for the Silver Cloud! One for invading *my* territory!" He noticed with satisfaction that the Chicago Bulls top was covered in mud and grass stains.

"Ow, ow!" the boy began to whimper, putting his arms up to protect his head.

"Alexander! Alexander!" At the sound of the familiar voice, both boys leapt up guiltily.

"Aunt Rhoda!" gasped the American.

"Mrs Granny!" Steven whispered at the same time. He looked up, over the grassy bank to the garden and the house beyond it. The house and the caravan site in Scotland had belonged to Mrs Granderton for as long as Steven could remember. He hadn't heard her come out of the house. He suspected the other boy hadn't either. Now she hobbled to the end of the garden and leaned on the wall.

"There you are, Alexander. And you, too, Steven!" She paused, coughing, but as she glanced from one to the other, her sharp eyes missed nothing. "I see you've already met. Let me introduce you properly. Alexander, this is Steven MacGregor, my right-hand man. His father is my warden. Mr MacGregor runs the site for me, and keeps me in order."

Steven stood up tall. He felt proud to be called a right-hand man.

"This is Alexander Curtis," she told Steven. "He's come to stay with me for a while, with his parents. His father, Jonathan, is a distant relative of my mother's, so I guess Alexander and I are third cousins or something!"

Steven turned to look at Alexander now. He was scowling and still breathing heavily. What's more, he had two black eyes. They weren't black yet, but they would be by tomorrow.

"But I thought you said ..." Steven began, turning back to Mrs Granderton.

"I know, dear. I told you I didn't have any relatives. It's what I always thought. Jonathan and his family have been living in America. They traced me through our family tree."

She swayed a little, and Steven jumped over the wall to hold her elbow and steady her.

"Thank you, dear," she said. Then she called to the other boy, "Come on now, Alexander, and wash your hands. Your mother has made dinner for us." She turned to smile at Steven. "You, too, dear. I expect it's your meal time soon." She lowered her voice so only Steven could hear. "Off you go, dear. I'll be all right now. I'll see you tomorrow."

Reluctantly, Steven climbed back over the wall. He'd noticed recently that Mrs Granderton was becoming wobbly, and she got out of breath easily. She had an outdoor sort of face, weathered and pink, but it was pale and thin these days. It made her dark eyes pop. She'd always been so active and busy, 'bustly', Mum called it, but now, with a stoop, she was slow and not much taller than Steven himself. Her trousers and fleecy jacket looked a size too big for her. Her hair was only just beginning to go grey, and she wasn't *that* old. Probably sixty-something. His mum said that wasn't really old at all.

Steven picked up the Silver Cloud's rope, and Alexander picked up his bike. Each avoided meeting the other one's eyes.

Steven was worried about Mrs Granderton, and puzzled about the Curtis family, but most of all, he was proud! His eye throbbed, but his heart sang! He had won the fight! At least, he had been winning, when Mrs Granderton called. Alexander was bigger, but he, Steven, had been on top. Two to one. A resounding victory!

He jogged home down the lane, the Silver Cloud clattering behind him, and a big grin spreading across his face. The cottage came into sight. There was a light on in the kitchen. Steven began to think of food. He broke into a run, but moved to the side of the road as he heard the familiar throb of his dad's van. Dad smiled and gave him a thumbs up signal as he passed, and began to indicate to pull into the cottage driveway. But as he did so, a smooth, fast car came from the opposite direction, round the bend, on the wrong side of the road. There was a screech of brakes, and the dreadful sound of metal scraping on metal, as the car's bumper scratched all along the side of the van.

Steven started forward, but stopped as a big man got out of the car. Steven gaped. The man was smiling! Dad got out of the van, tight-lipped, but self-controlled.

"Alan MacGregor, I presume?" he asked with an American drawl. "Jonathan Curtis. Relative of Rhoda Granderton." He stretched out his hand. Dad didn't shake it.

"Oh, don't worry about that," he said, nodding towards the scratched van. "It's hardly noticeable. We'll sort it out later. Anyhow," he added, still smiling, "it'll match the dent on the wing!" Steven was horrified. Hardly noticeable? It would take Dad days to knock that out and repaint it. It was true that the van wasn't smart. It had a few small dents and scratches, but this was by far the worst. Surely Dad must have wanted to punch the man on the nose! No! Dad was patient and polite. Rock-like. He'd never explode, even if he swallowed a stick of dynamite! His weathered face was a bit paler than usual, that was all. He pushed his dark hair out of his eyes.

After a few more words, which Steven couldn't really hear, the big man got back into his car, and Dad got into the van, and they drove on.

Steven ran into the drive, and caught up with his dad in the cottage doorway. "Dad! That man was driving on the wrong side of the road! It was all his fault! Why didn't you tell him? I could tell him! Let me do it!"

"Don't worry. We'll sort it out between us on the insurance. He's American. They drive on the right.

It probably slipped his memory," Dad replied mildly, opening the back door.

"What slipped whose memory?" Steven's mum asked, looking up from the plug she was changing on the toaster.

"Mum! This stupid American bumped into Dad's van and scratched it all down one side!"

"Oh, no, Alan!" Mum said, looking up at Dad. She put the screwdriver down and stood up. "Show me!"

"Me too!" Lucy demanded, jumping up from the table where she was drawing. The whole family went out to inspect the damage.

"What a shame!" Mum reached up to give Dad a peck on the cheek.

"I can knock out dents!" Steven declared. "Let me do it!"

"The other guy should pay to have it mended, Dad!" Lucy declared, her green eyes flashing. "Do you know who it was?"

"Oh yes! I know all right. It was Mrs Granny's new relative, Jonathan Curtis!"

"But I've just met his wife, Anne-Marie," Mum exclaimed. "She seemed ever so nice. Really friendly. Said she's cooking for all of them this evening."

For Steven, the light suddenly dawned. Curtis! That was the name Mrs Granny had said. Jonathan Curtis. And Alexander Curtis. So that was the boy's dad! Sure enough, they were alike, with blond hair and blue eyes.

"He should've said sorry, Dad!" Lucy insisted, jumping up and down. Whenever she got excited, her face turned as red as her hair.

"He was bigger than me, little fire-ball!" Dad said to Lucy, laughing. He put his arm round her shoulders. "I don't want to get off on the wrong foot with Mrs Granny's relatives. Anyway, character is more important than fists! Mrs Granny would say, 'How many times did Jesus say we should forgive people?'"

Lucy scowled. "Seventy times seven," she admitted reluctantly.

They went back into the cottage. Steven had been trying to keep his head down, but Mum noticed his eye. "Steve! Whatever have you been doing?" She tilted his face towards the light. Steven knew that Mum and Dad didn't approve of fighting, so he was reluctant to admit what had happened. Even though Mum was small and slim, she could be fiery-tempered when she was annoyed. Dad always said it went with the red hair.

Lucy came to Steven's rescue. "It was the Silver Cloud," she put in quickly. "You fell off again, didn't you?"

Steven nodded, and grinned gratefully at Lucy. She was OK, really, for a sister.

"Did you *really* fall off the Silver Cloud?" Mum asked, looking at him hard.

"Yes. When I landed." It was true, but Steven knew it wasn't the whole truth. His conscience pricked him a bit.

"Alan, can't you help him invent some brakes?" Mum asked Dad.

"I can invent some, Mum," Steven assured her. "Let me do it."

But Mum continued, "Lucy, clear your things up, love. I need to set the table."

Steven glanced at Lucy's drawing. It was a red squirrel.

She stacked her things on a shelf. "Race you to Hooper's Reach, Steve," she challenged, her hand on the door knob.

"Uh," Mum groaned. "I don't know where you two get the energy. Don't be long! Dinner in ten minutes," she called after them as they sped out of the cottage and up the lane.

Chapter 2

Hooper's Reach

Steven was never short of energy. He never walked if he could run, but Lucy had a head start on him now. She sprinted up the lane and veered off through the gate and up the steep, twisting path between the caravans. Despite being tired from cart-riding and fighting, Steven began to gain on her. She had never yet beaten him to the Reach. He was determined she never would, though she was pretty fast for a ten-year-old, and for a girl! He was glad he didn't have a sister who wore pink frills and didn't like getting dirty. She's like me, he thought, trying to lengthen his stride. She's not very tall, but she's strong, and she never seems to get tired!

He glanced for a moment to left and right. He could see that most of the caravans were empty, probably waiting for Easter, next weekend, when the holiday season started properly. He caught up with Lucy where the path forked. They ignored the left fork, because it only led along the top of the site, and back down the other side, reaching the lane beyond Mrs Granderton's house. Instead, they took the right fork, which led to the Reach. They ran past the last three caravans and arrived, hot and breathless, at a humpy, grassy area which overlooked the caravan site. They leaned on the fence, panting and laughing. The fence was sturdy, made of logs. Steven was proud of it because he and his dad had built it together.

"I'll beat you one day," Lucy challenged. "You'll get older and heavier, and I'll be slim and fast!"

"All my weight will be muscle, like Dad's," Steven retorted. "You'll wear a tight skirt and high heels and you won't be able to run!"

"Aye right!" said Lucy, turning to thump him, but when she noticed his closed eye, she said, "I'll not punch you. You've already lost one fight today. Right?"

"Wrong! I won! You should see the other guy!"

"It was that American boy, Curtis, wasn't it?"

"What are you, psychic or something? How did you know?"

"Mum was round at Mrs Granny's," Lucy said thoughtfully, fiddling with the end of her pony tail. "She met Mrs Curtis. She said she was very sweet, and Mum loved her accent! The Curtises have got a laptop. Mrs Curtis has got it set up on Mrs Granny's kitchen table."

"Mrs Granny thought she didn't have any relatives," Steven commented.

"She had us!"

"Yes, but ..." Steven didn't need to explain. Lucy knew Mrs Granderton wasn't really related to them, but they had grown up with her, and Steven had called her Mrs Granny before he could pronounce her name. She liked it, so it stuck.

They gazed out over the caravan site to the fields beyond, and finally to a flickering ribbon of silvery sea, glinting in the pale moonlight. Steven liked this time of the evening. It was growing dark now, and street lights twinkled along the coast road. A few of the privately owned caravans had lights on.

"Thing is," Lucy said quietly, "Mr Curtis told Mrs Granny to add more caravans. Said the site had lots more space. Said she could get lots more money for the best views."

"How do you know?"

"Mrs Granny told Mum."

"She won't though, will she! She's always said you should let the land breathe. Hooper's Reach was *her* special place when she was younger. Now it's ours!" He looked around the area where they were standing. Mrs Granny had told them it used to be woodland long ago, before she had owned the site. Someone had cut some of the trees down. The area was as big as a football field, but a funny shape. More like a star. Each point was surrounded by trees, and the furthest part was all woodland. It was the highest point of Mrs Granny's land. She told Steven she loved it for the views, the peace and the wildlife.

"We mustn't ever build on this bit, or put caravans on it," Mrs Granny had told him when he was small. "We mustn't drive the animals and birds away. God gave *us* homes, and he gave *them* homes, too. Let's not crowd them out. We must let the land breathe."

"No, she won't let them put caravans on Hooper's Reach," Steven tried to reassure himself. "It was her suggestion to bury Big Ears up here. She said he'd never be disturbed." He glanced towards his rabbit's grave, but a cold uncomfortable seed of fear took root in his heart.

"Come on, it'll be dinner time. I'm hungry," said

Lucy. "Ask Mum if there are any peas in the freezer. Get her to put a packet on your eye!"

"I'll find some," Steven replied. "I can do that."

The next morning was Saturday. There were no late bedders in the MacGregor household. Steven woke up before it was light, bursting with energy. There was lots to do. He wasn't going to waste any of his school holiday by lying in bed.

He'd forgotten about his black eye until he pulled his T-shirt over his head, then he fingered it tentatively, and went to look in the mirror. The swelling had almost gone down, but his eyelid was deep pink, and his cheek-bone was bluey-purple. It was like a battle trophy. He smiled.

Downstairs, Lucy was crossing off the days until the Holiday Club, like an advent calendar. "Two more days to go!" she declared. "I'm going to do lots of crafts again this year."

"I saw people getting the church hall ready yesterday," Mum said. "Looks great."

"You'll be too old for the Holiday Club this year, Steve," Dad commented, "But there's plenty to do here. You won't have time to get bored!"

Steven grinned. "Give me any job, Dad. I can do it!" He loved getting the site ready, and anyway, he felt he had grown out of the Holiday Club.

"What are you going to do today, love?" Dad asked Mum.

"Rosie's coming from the village at eight o'clock to help me check the equipment in the caravans," Mum replied. "Let's aim for a break at ten. I'll have the kettle on."

By seven o'clock, breakfast was eaten and cleared

away, and Dad, Steven and Lucy were at the top of the site. They began by mending and painting signposts: 'To Reception', 'To the showers', 'To caravans A1 to B10', and so on. Dad made sure that Steven and Lucy hammered nails in straight. Then they put a coat of paint onto the weathered letters. Steven admired Lucy's handiwork. She always painted neatly and carefully, never going over the edges, while he was usually in too much of a hurry.

At ten o'clock, as they walked home down the Silver Cloud's track, Jonathan Curtis came into sight. "Who's that, Dad?" Lucy asked. "The season hasn't started yet!"

Dad looked up. "Ah! That's Mr Jonathan Curtis, Mrs Granny's new relative."

Although Steven had to admit that Mr Curtis was tall and striking, with neatly-brushed blond hair, he also noticed there was no engine oil on his trousers, or holes in the elbows of his sweater.

Not a man for *real* work, he thought scornfully.

"Morning!" said Alan MacGregor heartily. "You haven't met my children. This is Steven."

Steven said "Hello," and felt himself blushing.

"And this is Lucy." Lucy put on one of her angelic smiles. Steven tried not to grin. Lucy's smile could charm the whiskers off a kitten, but he knew that the *real* Lucy could be as mischievous as an imp! "Children, this is Mr Curtis."

"Hi kids!" drawled Jonathan Curtis. He looked at Steven. "I gather you've already met my boy, Alexander?"

"Yes, I, er …"

"Isn't Alexander with you this morning, Mr Curtis?" Lucy asked sweetly, making a big show of looking round for him.

"Ah, no, not this morning, honey. He's not feeling too good. Decided to stay in."

"Oh, I'm sorry to hear that," Lucy said in her politest tone.

"Well, it's tea break for the workers," Alan MacGregor announced. He nodded to Jonathan Curtis, and headed towards the cottage. Steven and Lucy followed a few paces behind, holding their breath. When Mr Curtis was no longer in earshot, they exploded into guilty laughter.

"Alexander's a wimp!" Steven giggled. He mimicked Mr Curtis: "He's not feeling too good today!" He fingered his battle trophy. "Too afraid to show his two black eyes, more like! Cool line of questioning, Lucy!" He copied the way Lucy had looked around innocently for him.

"What's the joke, you monkeys?" Dad grinned, turning round.

Lucy and Steven looked at each other. "Er, nothing, Dad!"

In the cottage, Mum was pouring tea, and Rosie, already hot and puffed, was setting cups on the table.

"Hi kids!" Rosie said, as soon as Steven and Lucy arrived at the back door. "Seen our Kenny on your travels?"

"Kenny? Er – no. Is he …?" Steven began.

"He's coming to help your mum and me clean the caravans today, to earn some pocket money."

"Pocket money!" Steven said, pouring a glass of juice. "Can I clean for some pocket money? Let me do it – it's easy!"

"Clean? You?" Mum laughed. "You could wash your hands for a start." Steven sighed and went to the sink. What was the point of washing when you were going to get dirty again in five minutes?

"Anyway, you get paid plenty, Steven," Dad chuckled.

"Me? I never get paid a penny!"

"Well, let's see," said Dad. "There's free use of a huge play area, bigger than any of your school friends have." He counted on his fingers. "Then there's a challenging downhill slalom for the Silver Cloud, the best views in the country, your own wildlife park, an extra set of ready-made pals and the choice of a dozen hot showers!"

"I'm not bothered about the showers, but I guess the rest will do," Steven agreed, grinning.

"You got a pal coming then, Steve?" Rosie asked.

"Yeah. Graeme Robertson. His family owns a caravan. He helped us paint the Silver Cloud last season."

"Same age as you then, is he?"

"He's eleven. A year younger."

"It doesn't seem to matter, though," Mum put in. "Seems a very bright boy. Last year ..."

"Let me tell her, Mum," Steven objected. He turned to Rosie. "I told him how the bat boxes worked, and the tunnel for feeding the red squirrels so that the grey squirrels can't get at the food because they're too big. Graeme took it all in. He's quite clued-up, for a city kid."

"Steve, what did he write inside his Christmas card?" Lucy asked, grinning.

Steven quoted,

'If you want a good caravan site,
All you need is gas, sewage and light,
And of course, Steven's dad,
The best they've ever had,
'Cos he works his socks off day and night!'

They all laughed, and Rosie clapped.

"Do you think the Robertsons will be coming next weekend, Dad?"

" 'Spect so, son. I'll check the bookings when I go to Reception."

After a snack, Lucy said, "Can I check the folders, Mum? Dad said the zoo had sent new brochures."

"All right, love. But don't read every single one again. You'll be there all night."

"The quad bike centre gave us a new leaflet, too," Steven added.

"Right," said Mum. "And Lucy! If you find any of last year's information about the fisheries museum in the folders, take it out, because they've closed it this season."

"OK," Lucy agreed. "You coming, Steve?"

"No. I'm going to help Dad to check the power and plumbing."

Lucy went off happily to take out-of-date brochures out of the tourist information folders, and replace them with new ones.

Lucy loves paper, Steven thought. Reading, writing and drawing. Give me wood and nails, any time!

Everyone got up to go. There were several more long days of hard work ahead of them, Steven thought happily, before the site was ready for the beginning of the season. He shouldered his tool-bag and went out with his dad.

Chapter 3

Sparks Begin to Fly

By Wednesday, supplies had been checked, equipment listed, cleaning completed and gardening done. Steven and Lucy had put small welcome packs of tea, coffee, milk and matches in each caravan. In the late morning, Steven was so hot and thirsty, he burst into the cottage for a drink.

"Steven, pop round to Mrs Granny's with this fruit cake, and check she's OK, will you, love?" Mum begged.

"Do I have to, Mum?" He didn't want to run into Mr Curtis just now. "Anyway," he added, "that cake's too big. Why don't you cut her one slice, and we'll eat the rest?"

"It's for the whole family, silly," Mum said. "The Curtises as well. I'm trying to be friends."

"I don't think it's worth it, Mum. Mrs Curtis does lots of cooking. Anyway, I think *they* should be friends. After all, it was Jonathan Curtis who scraped Dad's van. And they seem to be trying to, kind of, take over."

"I know, love. But they're Mrs Granny's relatives. Her *only* relatives. If they're going to be here for a while, then I want to be friends with them. In any case, I think Mrs Granny might be pleased to see you."

"OK," Steven groaned, finishing his juice.

"If you see Dad, tell him it's lunch time."

"Last time I saw him, he was checking light bulbs in the showers," Steven called over his shoulder, already jogging out of the cottage.

Outside Mrs Granny's garden gate, Steven paused. He could hear his dad's voice, and someone else's, someone with an American accent. It must be Jonathan Curtis.

"Believe me, Mac," Mr Curtis was saying, "I'm a businessman. My cousin Rhoda is a sweet old dear, but she's out of touch. If she raised the rent and made a few alterations, she could strike it rich. She's sitting on a gold mine here!"

"Mrs Granderton sees value in other things, Mr Curtis, not just money. Her clients are happy and satisfied. She's not going to let them down."

Steven pictured them standing just outside Mrs Granny's back door. Suddenly he felt guilty, like he was eavesdropping on purpose. But he knew they'd stop talking if he showed himself, and this was important stuff. He wanted to hear it. He crouched down behind the wall, hardly daring to breathe in case he missed anything.

"That's because she didn't realise, doesn't realise, how she could develop the place," Mr Curtis was saying. "She could build a clubhouse. Hold discos from time to time. Attract young people."

Steven shifted his position and a stone crunched under his foot. He held his breath, but the voices continued as before.

"She works in co-operation with the people from the village, Mr Curtis. There's a youth club in the village: table tennis, snooker, that kind of thing.

They hold discos or ceilidhs, er... evenings of Scottish music and dancing, on a Saturday night, turn and turn about."

"She can't advertise that on her brochures of the site though, can she! And she needs a shop. Better still, a pizza bar. Create some employment for the locals. Make the place really buzz."

"The locals already have employment. There's a chippy in the village. It sells pizzas *and* Chinese food. And the supermarket sells everything. If we took away their customers, we'd lose a few friends," Steven's dad assured him grimly.

"You're being defeatist, Mac, and you know it! Rhoda could develop that land at the top of the site to a high standard. Best views, higher rent."

"That would make the site overcrowded." Steven could hear that his dad was getting impatient. "All the facilities cater for a maximum of one hundred caravans, including overnighters: tourers, tents and so on. The rubbish bins are hidden behind shrubs, there are bottle banks and paper collection points ..."

"I'm sure it would be no problem to fit a few more of those in," Mr Curtis interrupted.

"But overcrowding discourages wildlife," Steven's dad continued, "And creates all sorts of problems. We're very conservation conscious here, you know. Mrs Granderton does her best to keep the site friendly to the environment."

"Yeah! I did a project on that at school!" Steven stood up in surprise. That was Alexander's voice. What a creep! What was he doing there?

"Yep!" said Mr Curtis. "This young man per-suaded the whole school to use low-energy light bulbs. He even won a prize."

"Good on you, Alexander," Dad's voice had warmed. "We use them here, too, in the shower block and the reception chalet. Did your school use eco-friendly cleaning stuff, too?"

"I don't know about that, sir," Alexander replied.

Alexander sounded quite normal. Steven's anger died down to no more than a candle flame. A boy who could persuade his whole school to be more friendly to the environment couldn't be a total wimp after all. Steven decided to go through the gate and join in.

"We always use cleaning materials that cause less pollution," his dad was saying.

"Yeah," Steven agreed, walking up to stand beside his dad. "And we have nesting boxes, and bat boxes, and a tunnel for feeding the red squirrels." Everyone had turned towards him. "And we use recycled paper for our advertising, and we leave areas of grass unmown so the wild plants can grow. We make sure that ..."

"Woah, little guy! It sounds like you need to stop for breath!" Jonathan Curtis laughed.

Steven looked from one to the other. Alexander wasn't laughing at him. Dad was nodding in agreement. Only Mr Curtis seemed to think he'd said something funny, though if he had, he couldn't imagine what it was.

"Well," Jonathan Curtis drawled, "it looks like Rhoda has you working all round the clock. Time she paid you a fair wage." He took a step towards Alan MacGregor to press his point home. "If we went ahead with these developments ..."

"I'm not complaining about my wages," Alan MacGregor said, his voice crisp and tight. "I've always ..."

"At least then," Mr Curtis interrupted, "you could buy your boy a decent bike, instead of letting him endanger himself *and* my son with his crate on wheels!"

Steven's anger flared back up to a raging fire. He looked around. Dad was angry, too. His face turned first red, then white. Steven wanted to thump Mr Curtis. He wanted to see those neatly pressed cream trousers covered in mud. He longed to ... But Dad was speaking: "Come on, Steven, there's work to be done." His voice was quiet and controlled. He put his hand on Steven's shoulder.

"But I'm supposed to ... Mum asked me ..."

"What, son?"

"Mum's sent this cake for Mrs Granny." But the last thing he wanted to do just now was to go into the house with the Curtises, while Dad walked home to the cottage.

"Come on then, little guy, she'll be glad to see you," Mr Curtis said, putting a hand on Steven's other shoulder. Steven wriggled away from the big hand and followed Alexander into the house.

"Mom?" Alexander called in the hall. "Mom, Steven's come."

Mrs Curtis appeared from the kitchen. She looked smart enough for a party, even though she'd probably been cooking. "Hi honey! How nice to meet you!" She held out a hand. Steven shook it. He was surprised and relieved. He'd half expected her to tell him off for fighting and messing up

Alexander's clothes. Instead, she was smiling warmly.

"Er, my mum sent this cake for Mrs Granny, er, and for all of you," he explained.

"Oh, that is so sweet of her!" Mrs Curtis exclaimed, taking a peek inside the tin. "I love fruit cake. I'm sure Mrs G will be so pleased to see you. In there, honey." She pointed to the front room, and she and Alexander disappeared into the kitchen.

Steven put his head round the door. Mrs Granny was sitting by the window, but she wasn't looking out. She was staring down at the floor. She looked miserable. Steven wondered how much of the argument she had overheard.

"Hello, Mrs Granny." He stepped hesitantly into the room. He didn't usually feel shy, but today Mrs Granny looked so unhappy, and her pleasant, open face was quite grey. She beamed when she saw him though, and patted the chair next to her for him to sit down.

"Mum's sent this fruit cake." He set the tin down on the coffee table.

"Oh, lovely, dear. Please say thank you to her for me. I do love your mother's cakes." She leaned forward and whispered, "Anne-Marie's cooking is very posh. It's too rich for me, I'm afraid." Steven nodded. He guessed Mrs Granny didn't eat much of it.

He couldn't think of anything to say, so he looked round the room. As always, he gazed at the MacGregor shield and sword. It was a kind of joke between him and Mrs Granny. One of her ancestors had been a MacGregor, and had fought battles with the shield and sword that hung on the wall. They were beautifully mounted on a square of MacGregor tartan – bold red with a green stripe. When Steven was very small, he'd asked if he could have them. She had chuckled, and said they should be his, really, because he was a true MacGregor. Then she had become serious, and said he was too young for them now, but they would become his one day.

She saw him looking, now. "Yes, they'll be yours eventually, Steven. I suppose those mean that your family and I are distantly related, way back," she said.

"But the Curtises are not so distant ...?" He made it sound like a question.

"So it seems, dear, so it seems," she said vaguely. "They're keen on history. I think a lot of Americans are. They looked up our family tree. My mother was a distant relative of Jonathan's father. I'm their only Scottish relative, so, of course, I invited them to stay."

Steven took a breath to ask more, but he didn't know what to ask. It seemed so strange, the Curtises turning up out of the blue.

"Now, Steven," Mrs Granny said, back to her real, business-like self. "There's something I'd like you to do for me. Would you go up to the Reach with me, this afternoon, if you're free?"

"Yes, of course, I can do that. But it's rather ..."

"I know, dear. It's a long, steep walk. I was wondering if your father would take me up in the van as far as the top caravan. I could walk the last few yards."

"Yes, I'm sure he would. I'll ask him. I ought to

go, now, Mrs Granny."

"Yes, of course. Off you go, dear. It's very nice to see you." Mrs Granny smiled, and Steven stood up. Then she added, "Tell your mum not to worry. I'll be all right."

Steven said "OK," and left by the back door. He heard her coughing as he went.

The moment he was outside, he thought about the argument again. Something was niggling at the back of his mind. Something about Alexander. He went over what Mr Curtis had said about the Silver Cloud. He'd called it a crate on wheels. Fiery anger burned up inside him again at the memory. He rode the Silver Cloud because it was more interesting than a bike. Of course he had a bike, though not a posh one like Alexander's. But bikes had brakes. They were boring and safe. He used his bike to fetch shopping from the village for Mum. But he had made the Silver Cloud himself.

He tried to remember Jonathan Curtis's exact words. 'If he had a bike, he wouldn't put himself *and* my boy in danger with his crate on wheels!'

Yes! That was it! Slowly, Steven realised what that meant. Mr Curtis thought his son had fallen off the Silver Cloud! So Alexander hadn't gone home and whimpered about Steven hitting him. So he hadn't told his dad about the fight. Steven's opinion of him was definitely getting better.

Suddenly Steven realised he was standing still. He'd forgotten to tell Dad it was lunch time, and that was ages ago. He sprinted home down the lane to the cottage.

Chapter 4
Back to Hooper's Reach

"Why do you think Mrs Granny wants to go to the Reach this afternoon, Dad?" Steven asked after lunch.

"I'm not sure, son. I don't think she's been up there for a while. The sun's shining. The views will be smashing today." Dad paused. "Steve, you know Jonathan Curtis is pressing her to develop the Reach for more caravans, don't you?"

"Yes, I overheard. But she won't agree, will she?"

"I hope not. It would go against all she stands for, everything that's become important to all of us during the last few years. But ..."

"But what?"

"I don't know, son. Things are a bit different now."

"How different? The Curtises are here, but they're not going to be here for ever!"

Alan MacGregor was silent.

"They *aren't*, are they, Dad?"

"I don't know. They've been looking at houses in the village. Mr Curtis seems to be an experienced businessman. He may not be very good at getting his hands dirty, but he has done very well in the States. He knows how to build up a business, and how to expand it and make it successful. He's try-ing to persuade Mrs Granny to take him on.

To employ him."

"But this isn't the States, Dad. This is Scotland."

"I know, son. But maybe I've been missing opportunities all this time. I wouldn't know. I'm OK at mending fences and unblocking toilets, even buying caravans. But as for the rest …"

Steven had never seen him look so fed up. "You're fantastic, Dad!" he objected, jumping up and hugging him briefly. "Mr Curtis could never have helped anyone build a Silver Cloud, or make a hide for bird-watching, or help the vet when Farmer Mackay's cow was having her calf! Or mend the van, or pitch tents, or build a tree house, or …"

"OK, son! Thanks for cheering me up." Dad was laughing now. "Let's go and pick up Mrs Granny."

Mrs Granny was standing at her front door waiting, when they arrived. "Sorry to be a nuisance, Alan," she said as Dad helped her into the van, "Especially at such a busy time. It was just a whim, I suppose."

"No problem, Mrs G. I've brought my tools, anyway, because there's a couple of jobs to do on caravans B7 and B8."

He parked the van as near as he could to the Reach, and he and Steven took one of her arms each, and walked with her to the top. The short walk made her gasp and cough, so Steven found a log for her to sit on. While she got her breath back, the three of them gazed out over the caravan site, then past Farmer Mackay's meadows to the glittering blue sea. The only sound was a faint whisper of breeze stirring the young leaves in the trees behind them. Mrs Granny sighed with pleasure. "It's just as good as I'd always remembered it!" She smiled and put a hand on Steven's shoulder. The fresh air had brought a hint of colour to her cheeks, and she looked more like the Mrs Granny who used to play hide-and-seek among the caravans with Steven and Lucy. Or who had stood with Dad on the site, come wind or rain, making decisions about the placement of caravans. Or who had marched solemnly up to the Reach for Big Ears' funeral.

"I'm off for a couple of minutes," Dad said, opening the back of the van and humping his tool-bag on to his shoulder.

"Look, Mrs Granny! I've put the hide up again!" Steven bounded to the shelter, twenty metres behind them. He had rigged it up out of sticks and an old tent to watch birds so that they weren't aware of him. "It blew down in the gales, but I put it up again last week."

"Great, Steven! Well done. And what have you seen?"

"Chaffinches, sparrows, thrushes, and one day the green woodpecker was here again. In that tree. Over there!" Steven pointed.

"You could hang up some bacon fat and peanuts," Mrs Granny suggested. "Make a string pulley between those two trees, and hoist the food up between the two, so the grey squirrels can't get it, then you might see some blue tits and nuthatches."

"OK. I can do that. I'll ask Mum for some bacon."

Mrs Granny turned back to look at the sea and the sunny blue sky. Steven came and sat on the ground beside her.

36

"Mrs Granny? Do you want to put caravans up here?" He'd been burning to ask the question. "People say you could charge a high rent for such good views."

"Don't pay any attention to the gossip. This site is big enough. If we added any more caravans, we'd have to cut more trees down, and then we'd lose some wild-life habitats. God has *lent* the planet to us. It's not ours to waste and spoil. He tells us to look after it for him. He's the chief gardener, or the site manager, if you like!" She chuckled for a moment. "And we're the wardens. He'll come back to see what sort of a job we've made of it. Let's not spoil the beauty. We've got to let the land breathe. It's one thing to listen to what other people think, but once you've made up your mind ..." She tailed off, deep in thought. Steven was relieved. Nothing was going to change. He wondered how long she was going to sit there.

"Steven? Do you ever think of heaven?" she asked suddenly.

"Er ..."

"What do you think it'll be like?" she insisted.

"Pretty much like this, I suppose," said Steven, looking round. It was his favourite place on earth.

"I'm certain it'll be beautiful," Mrs Granny agreed warmly. "But it'll be full of people, too. People who belong to God. There won't be any pollution, or greed." She paused, then added, "Or fighting!" She looked sideways at Steven, with a twinkle in her eye. He grinned sheepishly. Then she stood up slowly and leaned on the wooden fence. "And it'll last for ever!" she finished triumphantly.

Steven felt full of questions. He wanted to know what Mrs Granny was going to say to Jonathan Curtis. He wondered whether she even liked her relatives, especially Alexander. He wanted to ask her why she coughed so much and got tired so quickly, and why she was suddenly thinking of heaven. But she was so quiet and peaceful, and this moment seemed too special to spoil with his questions. So he leaned on the fence beside her and tried to think only about good things: about Graeme Robertson, and the Silver Cloud, and school holidays. About the green woodpecker, and the song thrushes ...

"Madam, your carriage awaits!" Steven's dad announced with a low bow and a big grin.

"Why, I thank you, my man!" replied Mrs Granny, bowing her head slightly, and grinning back.

Dad offered his arm, and Steven did the same. "Let me help! I can do that!" Again she took an arm on each side, and was escorted back to the van. They chatted and laughed, like old times, and the special moment became just a memory.

At the bottom of the hill, Dad stopped the van and said to Steven, "Out you get, son. I'm just going to take Mrs Granny on one more errand, then we'll finish the plumbing."

"Where are you going, Dad?"

"Oh, just into the village," Dad said vaguely. "See you shortly."

That night Steven woke suddenly. He didn't know what had disturbed him. The cottage was dark and silent. He lay staring into the blackness and heard a distant owl hoot. After a while there was an answering call. He got out of bed and opened his curtains a bit. The moon was bright and almost full. All the caravans were in darkness. He looked towards the Reach. The stars twinkled down on the dark mass of forest. He didn't feel tired at all, but he did feel thirsty. He pulled on a warm sweater over his pyjamas, and found his socks. He tiptoed down to the kitchen and poured himself a glass of apple juice.

Leaning on the kitchen window sill, he watched the Reach. An occasional winged shape cast a shadow in the moonlight, and Steven longed to be out there, enjoying the night sounds.

The stairs creaked, and Steven looked behind him. A face peered round the door. "Dad! You scared me! What are you doing down here?"

"I was going to ask you the same question!" Dad grinned.

"I was thirsty. Came for some juice. Hey, Dad! Look at the moon shining on the Reach! Isn't it cool! I wish I was up there. The badgers might be out."

Dad came to stand beside him at the window and they gazed up the hill. An idea struck Steven, and he was sure it struck his dad at the same time. They looked at each other.

"Can we go, Dad?"

"Now?"

"Yes! Please!"

Dad looked him up and down. "Put your jeans and trainers on, and I'll get my joggers and jacket."

Two minutes later they crept noiselessly out of the cottage, and set off up the hill at a gentle jog.

They paused beside the last empty caravan to get their breath back before arriving at the Reach. They didn't want to scare away any animals or birds by puffing and panting. When they were ready, they crept up to the fence and looked out. The sea was a ghostly silver ribbon in the moonlight. A single car drove along the coast road. Steven could just hear the hum of its distant engine. Then all was silent. With the empty space and the dark trees behind them, Steven felt they were being watched. The hair on the back of his neck prickled. He listened so hard, his ears began to buzz.

Steven loved the scary feeling. This is why people pay lots of money for roller-coaster rides, he thought. He had only been once. He remembered the terror which squeezed his heart as he waited for the carriage to start. Then came the wide-mouthed silent scream which filled his head as he rushed downhill at suicidal speed. And he remembered the tidal wave of pride when he'd done it. He used to be scared of the dark when he was little. He always asked Mum to leave the landing light on. He remembered when Mrs Granny had been his Sunday School teacher. She had told the children to ask Jesus to help them when they were scared. Steven had done that. It must have worked, he thought suddenly, because he didn't need the light on now! Or maybe he'd just grown out of it.

But now it was fun being scared. Exciting. He held his breath and shivered in delight. Behind them, a scuffling and snuffling began. He turned his head slowly, fingers of fear playing tunes up and down his spine. Behind them, the darkness was much more dense, so he waited a moment for his eyes to get used to it.

Slowly, so slowly, they made their way to his hide. It was only twenty metres away but it took minutes. They put each foot down carefully, deliberately, eager not to tread on twigs that might crack. Steven was grateful for a gentle sigh of breeze from the woods. It covered the sound of his breathing and the knocking of his heart, and it carried the good familiar smell of pine trees.

In the hide, they found comfortable positions and peered through the look-out slit. For a long time they saw nothing. Steven shifted his position without making a sound. Then suddenly, Dad gripped his arm and pointed. Their patience was rewarded. With a gentle swoosh, a barn owl landed on a branch only metres from the hide. Steven caught the shine of silver-grey wing feathers in the moonlight, and watched, breathless, as it swivelled its head round a complete circle. For a moment it seemed to look straight at him. It was beautiful.

Then something alarmed it, and it took off, gliding noiselessly, above his head. Steven peered all around to see what had surprised the owl. He caught his breath in amazement. Just ahead of them, out of a well-disguised set, plodded a family of badgers, snuffling and grunting. Dad had told him he thought there was a set somewhere, but Steven had never seen badgers on the Reach before. He stared, spell-bound, as they rooted for food. He gasped with delight as two of the cubs rolled over each other in a rough-and-tumble game, like a pair of boisterous puppies. Then the big heavy mother badger trundled along to keep them in order, and the family disappeared into the woodland to look for their supper.

Steven wanted to shout and run and jump. Just wait till I tell Lucy, he thought. Then he checked himself. Better not tell Lucy. She'll want to come, too. No, it would be their own secret. His and Dad's. Maybe later, he'd tell Graeme. But not straight away.

Realising he was cold and stiff, Steven thought of his warm bed. Creeping quietly out of the hide, they jogged on light feet down the path, back to the cottage. They tiptoed back upstairs and whispered goodnight to each other. Stripping off his clothes, Steven got into bed. Although he was sure he wasn't tired, he pulled the warm covers up to his chin, and didn't remember anything more.

Chapter 5

Making Plans

Sometime in the early morning, Steven woke suddenly. He was sweating, and his throat was dry. Something was making his heart thud. Then his dream came flooding back. He'd been trying to run to the Reach, but he couldn't get past the top caravan. His feet were running on the spot. The Reach was in danger. His hide and the badgers' set were being destroyed by something big and loud. He was shouting for it all to stop, but no-one could hear him over the noise. Angry and frightened, Steven shivered, even though he was sweating. He swallowed to try to ease his throat. In the dream, there was no-one to help. It was all up to him.

Steven lay very still to calm himself, and tried to think clearly about the situation. Gradually a plan formed in his mind. A chink of grey light filtered through his curtains, and he could hear noises from the kitchen. It must be morning. He jumped out of bed and drew his curtains back. Up at the Reach, the pine trees stood peaceful and majestic as always. There, in the early morning, Steven made a promise. He whispered it, instead of just thinking it, to make it more real. "I will *not* let them put caravans on the Reach. I will *not* let the badgers be killed, or any of the other creatures that live up there. And I will *not* let anyone disturb Big Ears' grave. I can do it."

He couldn't see Mrs Granny's house from the cottage, but he turned in the direction of it and whispered, "I'll look after the Reach for you, Mrs Granny. I'll make them let the land breathe."

Afterwards, feeling calm and determined, and full of his usual energy, he ran downstairs for breakfast.

It was Good Friday. Dad had made bacon and eggs for breakfast. "Dad, are you going to give Mrs Granny a lift to church?" Steven asked, buttering toast.

"I don't think she's feeling up to it, son. She said yesterday that she'd probably stay in and watch the service on television."

"Dad, what's wrong with Mrs Granny? She's not *that* old."

"I'm not rightly sure, son. She never really got over the bronchitis she had in the winter."

"Well it's spring now, so maybe she'll get better!"

"I hope so, son. Now I must go and check the stocks in reception. By the way, the Robertsons are arriving this afternoon."

"Cool!" Steven leapt up. "I'll go and get the Silver Cloud out before Graeme comes round." He ran out to the shed, but there was something he had to do first. It was part of THE PLAN. He wheeled his bike out into the yard, and found Dad's metal cleaner. Then he polished his bike wheels till they were as shiny as possible, and wiped over the framework with a damp cloth. The bike was not as flash as Alexander's, of course, but the wheels sparkled when he turned them fast.

He rode his bike down the lane and into the gate of the site. He rode up and down the path outside Mrs Granny's garden, gathering speed, and finally coming to a halt in a well-controlled skid on some loose gravel. Mrs Curtis appeared at Mrs Granny's back door. She smiled broadly when she saw Steven, and waved. She went back into the house, and soon afterwards Alexander appeared, but Steven pretended not to notice because he wanted the chance to show Alexander a thing or two first. Then he rode as fast as he could, skidding, making a figure of eight, zooming downhill no-handed, and showing off all the tricks he knew. Finally, Alexander came out of the gate. He stood on the grassy bank and called "Hi."

Steven pretended to be very surprised to see him, but skidded impressively to a halt. He whipped a spanner out of his back pocket. "Hi," he said, unscrewing the saddle quickly and expertly. "Need to alter the suspension for this mixed terrain," he added, taking the saddle off, trying the springs, fiddling a bit, and screwing it back on again with nimble fingers. He wiped his oily hands on the seat of his jeans, the way his dad always did. "Won't be able to ride the Silver Cloud once the site fills up. Have to resort to the bike."

"Oh!" said Alexander, obviously impressed.

"Should have brought one of my other spanners," Steven added casually.

"You got your own tools?" Alexander asked enviously.

"Yep." He treasured them because Mrs Granny had given them to him for his eleventh birthday.

"Cool! Wish I had. Aunt Rhoda has a beautiful box of tools ..."

"... in the cupboard under the stairs." Steven knew because she'd shown them to him.

"Yeah."

"I hear your dad wants to put caravans on the high ground?" Steven said casually.

"Yeah. Hooper's Reach. My great-grandfather was called Mr Hooper. My family came from Scotland, you know." Then he added, "Good views up there."

Great-grandfather, eh? Steven thought. I suppose that he'll be claiming he owns the land, next! But he fiddled with his bike and said, "Not a good move."

"Why not?"

"Well, for a start, it's difficult to get a good water supply and sewage disposal working up there. It's gravity. It works against you."

"But there are plenty of houses on higher hills than this one," Alexander objected, "And they've got perfectly good drainage systems."

"Yes, but because a caravan site is only semi-permanent, and because the land has lots of rocky outcrops, the sewage system isn't sunk very deep. Could cause a problem." Aware that what he was saying was only half true, Steven felt himself blushing. But he hoped his cheeks were red anyway, from cycling in the cold air. Besides, everyone always said he looked permanently tanned. He was proud to look like a workman, not a pale-faced swot.

"Uh-huh," said Alexander thoughtfully.

"Have you looked round one of the caravans?" Steven asked.

Alexander shook his head.

"I'll show you one. Tomorrow morning. Haven't got time today. Lots of people arriving. I'll show you around the one at the top. It's not being used this week. Got to go now." He leapt on his bike and cycled off at top speed. "See ya!" he called over his shoulder.

Back at the cottage, Steven put away his bike and his spanner. He felt sure he had managed to convince Alexander that he knew what he was talking about.

In the afternoon, Steven helped his mum at the reception chalet. He leapt to the window at the sound of every car, longing for the Robertsons to arrive. When Graeme finally came striding up the chalet steps with his dad, Steven stared. Graeme was several centimetres taller than him. Rats! Why couldn't he grow!

"Hello," Graeme smiled.

"Hi."

"What are you staring at?"

"You! You've grown!"

"That's what the aunties and uncles are supposed to say, not you!"

"And where are your glasses?"

"I'm bionic! Contact lenses and a metal-mouth!" He grinned broadly to show off his teeth brace.

"And you!" Graeme added. "Cool hair cut! Where are your curls?"

"Grew out of them!"

The ice was broken, and they both laughed. Mr Robertson signed in and collected the keys.

"Dad, can I ... " Graeme began.

"Just help me unload the car, then you and Steven can go off together," Mr Robertson promised.

"Race you to the Reach!" said Steven as soon as Graeme reappeared. He set off at a gallop, with Graeme on his heels. He was relieved to find he was still faster, even though Graeme had longer legs.

At the top, they sat on the fence, their toes hooked under the lower rail, and looked out over the site. Steven told Graeme about the Curtises' arrival, about his fight with Alexander, about Mrs Granny being so unwell, and finally about Jonathan Curtis's plans to develop the Reach.

Graeme became serious as he listened, and his clear blue eyes grew wide. "What does your dad have to say about it?"

"He hates the idea, of course, but he can't really do anything, because Mrs Granny is his boss. And Jonathan Curtis is her relative."

"Could you say anything to Mr Curtis?"

"Nae. He just laughs at me and calls me a 'little guy'."

"OK. So it's up to us then."

Us! Steven sighed with relief. He wasn't on his own. Graeme was on his side, and he wasn't carrying the burden of his promise alone any more. "I've got a PLAN. Mr Curtis won't listen to me or Dad, but he *will* listen to Alexander."

"So we have to reach the father through the son," Graeme summed up.

"Right. I think we can do that. Listen!" Steven leaned towards Graeme, lowered his voice, and explained his PLAN in detail. "First, I'll have to show you a map of the site, and where the sewage outlets are. The maps are in Reception, but we'll have to wait till Dad's left and gone home, so he won't suspect anything."

"What about Lucy?" Graeme asked. "Are we going to let her in on it?"

"No," said Steven. "At least, not yet."

Chapter 6

Fliers, Spaghetti and Blocked Pipes

Steven stopped off to say hello to Graeme's mum and dad on his way home to the cottage. Although he knew that Graeme's dad was a city lawyer, he couldn't imagine him in a business suit. Steven had only ever seen him in jeans and a T-shirt. Graeme's dad was always friendly and welcoming, and he laughed a lot with a deep, warm voice. He seemed pleased to see Steven again.

Graeme's mum was quiet but friendly. She smiled and opened a packet of Jaffa cakes when the boys appeared. As she offered them around, she asked, "Have you lads made plans already, then?" Steven nearly choked on his Jaffa cake, trying not to laugh.

"We have!" said Graeme, very seriously.

After tea, Steven met up with Graeme again. "I've had an idea!" Graeme hissed excitedly. "We could make a flier. An advertisement. We could tell people about the wildlife, and our aims for the caravan site, and ask them to sign a petition if they don't want the site to be developed. They're sure to agree. The grown-ups like peace and quiet. They wouldn't want earth-movers on the site, or a disco!"

It wasn't part of his own plan, Steven reasoned,

but Graeme's ideas were usually worth having, so he said, "Yes! Let's do it!" He paused. "Er, how?"

"My dad's brought his lap-top: printer, scanner, the lot. Mum told him off. Said this was a holiday. But he brought them anyway."

"So he could print off whatever we asked him?"

"Yes. Or I could."

"Wow! Great!" said Steven. "So what shall we put?"

" 'Save our wildlife!' Then, er …."

"If you want peace and quiet to continue, er … No, er …" Steven frowned as he tried to think hard. "We need something snappy. Let's go to the cottage and get some paper to write ideas down." He leapt up.

Lucy was sitting at the kitchen table, drawing. "Hi Lucy!" Graeme said.

"Hi!" said Lucy, her mouth dropping open. She looked at Graeme just as Steven had done earlier, from his feet to the top of his head.

"Don't say it," Graeme laughed. "I've grown. Bet you have, too."

"I have!" Lucy stood up on her tiptoes to prove it. "Anyway, what are you two doing? What are you looking so steamed up about?"

"We're going to make a flier to take round the caravan owners …" Steven began.

"And the people in the rented caravans …" Graeme interrupted.

"… asking them to sign a petition if they don't want the site to be overdeveloped," Steven finished. "A petition. You know, a list of names of people who agree."

"I know what a petition is!" Lucy said scornfully.

"I told him what Mr Curtis said," Steven went on. Lucy nodded. "Mr Robertson's brought his lap- top, and Graeme could print fliers off for us."

"Great! And we could put the petition in reception," Lucy added. "So what are we going to write?" She took a pencil and a piece of paper from her folder.

"We're not sure yet. Any ideas?" Steven asked hopefully.

"How about, 'This site is under threat!'" Lucy began.

Graeme continued,

"'If you care about our wildlife,
    Badger, owl and pine,
    Our petition's in Reception,
    Please would you sign?'"

"Fantastic! And it needs pictures." Steven looked at Lucy.

"I could draw an owl in one corner ..."

"... and a badger in the other!" Steven finished.

So they sat at the kitchen table, and Lucy drew while Steven and Graeme planned out the words.

"We'll take them round and give them to people. I could do that!" Steven said, then paused. "Or you could, Graeme. People listen to you if your dad's a lawyer," he added. "Lucy could, too. Everyone thinks she's so polite and cute!"

"Yuk!" said Lucy, breaking off drawing to thump him.

"But you should most of all, Steve," Graeme said, "because everyone knows it's you and your dad who do the real work around here."

When it was finished, Steven asked, "Could you

do it first thing in the morning?"

"He could do it now," Lucy suggested. "It's not very late."

Steven looked at Graeme to warn him. He'd planned to take Graeme to Reception and show him the plans. He didn't think there'd be time to do the flier as well, but he didn't want Lucy to suspect anything. Graeme got the message. "I'll see ..." he faltered, "I'll see whether my dad's using the computer. Bye, Lucy." Steven grabbed the paper, and the two of them dashed out of the door. Graeme stuck his head back round. "Great drawings, Lucy. Thanks."

Steven's dad was arriving at the cottage just as they left. "Where are you two off to?" he asked.

"Oh, er, just around," Steven said.

"All right, but don't be too late. It's getting dusk already."

"OK Dad. I've got my torch."

They made off down the lane and through the gate on to the site. "Good. Dad's home. That means reception will be empty," Steven announced. He patted his pocket, where he had the spare key to the reception chalet. They looked around guiltily. Lots of the caravans had lights on, and some had their curtains drawn already, but there was no-one outside or walking through the site.

"Anyway, I'm allowed in reception," Steven whispered. Nevertheless, he felt like a criminal as they crept in and locked the door behind them, without putting the light on. Steven went to a filing cabinet in a little office behind the desk. He switched on his torch, and took out a large map of the site. He unfolded it and spread it out on the floor. He and Graeme knelt down and stared at it.

"Looks like spaghetti!" Graeme observed.

"The red lines show where electricity cables are laid," Steven explained, tracing some with his finger.

"Some of them end up nowhere!"

"Those are the sites reserved for tents and tourers. Some of them want to hook up to power. These blue ones, these are the sewage outlets."

"Ought to be brown!" Graeme burst out.

"Shh!" Steven warned him, and they giggled helplessly, rolling all over the map.

"Ah. As I thought," said Steven when they had pulled themselves together. He put his right first finger on the highest caravan, the last one before the Reach, and with his left, he traced the blue line that led down to the main outlet. "Look! This caravan, and the two next to it, have sewage pipes that join the main drains just here." He stabbed with his finger. "If there was a blockage here, just below this man-hole cover," he stabbed again, "all the sewage from these two would come up this one. These two are occupied this weekend, but this one isn't. So this is the one I'm going to show Alexander around." Satisfied, he sat back on his heels.

"A blockage? What sort of blockage?"

"We'll stop it up with a plug. I can do it. There'll be one here." He rummaged in a box of tools at the back of the little office.

"Looks like a giant's bath plug!" Graeme commented.

"It's what we use when we're working on one part of the system, but we don't want the rest to be affected," Steven explained.

"You mean, when they flush the toilet in this caravan ..." It was Graeme's turn to stab his finger at the map, "it all comes up this one!"

"Yep!" Steven grinned. "Don't worry. I can do it. In one night it won't be enough to make a mess. Just a pong ..."

"So we're going to take Alexander round the smelly one?"

"Yep!"

"Don't you think he'll rumble us?"

"Not a chance. I've managed to convince him I know what I'm talking about."

"And he'll tell his dad about the smell, and that'll begin to put him off the idea?" Graeme sounded doubtful.

"You've got it," Steven said feeling confident. He folded up the map carefully and put it back in the filing cabinet.

They jogged back to the cottage, and Steven opened the shed door quietly. He took out a pair of chunky iron keys to open the man-hole cover.

"All we need now is stocking face masks!" Graeme commented. "And if we're caught, it'll take more than my dad to defend us!"

"But it's all in a good cause," Steven assured him, as they made their way up the hill.

Quietly Steven inserted his man-hole cover key and showed Graeme how to do the same. They turned the keys and heaved the heavy cover off. Steven shone his torch and peered down.

"Ugh! Stinks!" They both came up for air.

"Look, see that pipe? Here, hold the torch, and keep a look out at the same time. If anyone comes, I'll say I've lost my ball down the hole." He took his jacket off and rolled up the sleeve of his sweatshirt. Then he reached inside, grunting, and rammed the plug into position. "There!" he said finally, sitting up. "That should do it." Together they replaced the man-hole cover.

Suddenly Steven giggled.

"What?"

"I was just remembering. Once, in the supermarket, when Lucy was little, she said to Mum, 'Don't buy recycled toilet paper!' She thought it had *already* been used as toilet paper!"

Chuckling, they made their way down to the nearest standing tap for the tents and tourers. Steven washed his hand and arm as thoroughly as he could, just in case. Then he said goodnight to Graeme, and trotted home to the cottage, windmilling his arm to dry it off.

Chapter 7

Skunks and Christmas Lights

On Easter Saturday morning, Steven took the key to the top caravan and went to hang around outside Mrs Granny's house. When Alexander appeared, Steven asked him, "Want to go and look around a caravan?"

"OK."

"We could go up to the one at the top. It's a lovely caravan and it's got a good view." Steven tried to speak like a salesman. Then he added, "As I explained, there's sometimes a problem with the sewage, because it's hard to pump enough fresh water up the hill to flush the toilet properly. But let's hope everything's OK today." As they walked up the hill, Steven told Alexander about the bird boxes, and some of the animals and birds he'd seen. He was careful to stress how timid the animals were, and how they didn't like to be disturbed.

They reached the caravan, and as Steven opened the door, a terrible smell hit them.

"Whoa! Skunks!" Alexander exclaimed.

"Oh dear," said Steven, "I wanted to show you what a lovely caravan it is."

"Maybe we should flush the toilet?" Alexander suggested.

"No!" said Steven quickly, imagining the whole

thing overflowing. "This is an underground job. Me and Dad'll do it later this morning."

With the caravan door wide open, the air improved enough for Steven to show Alexander all the caravan's modern luxuries. "It sure is comfortable," Alexander said, genuinely pleased. "My dad was planning to ask Mac to show him around a van today. Maybe we could show him instead? Er, one that doesn't smell?"

"Um, yes, of course!" The Plan was running a bit ahead of Steven. "You go and get your dad, and I'll get another key from reception."

They went separately downhill. As soon as Alexander was out of sight, Steven turned off towards Graeme's caravan. He found Graeme busy at the computer. "Can you spare a minute? Now? Important job on!"

Graeme said to his dad, "Please don't shut the computer down, Dad. I'm going to finish off as soon as I get back."

Outside, Steven asked, "Can you go to reception and get the key to A10? Ask my mum if it's all right to show the Curtises round?"

"But I thought we were going to wait for a windy day to show Mr Curtis round," Graeme objected. "Then we could blame the electrics on the wind ..."

"No time!" Steven panted. "Alexander said his dad was going to ask my dad for a tour. If he did, we'd lose our chance."

"What are *you* going to do?"

"Got to unblock the drains. If the two other caravans have problems with their toilets, they'll tell my dad. And when he discovers the cause, then

I'll be the one with the problems!" Steven chuckled darkly. "And delay Alexander if you can."

"But I've never even met him!"

"Oh, er, go and get Lucy!" Steven pleaded. He felt so wound up he couldn't keep still.

"OK," Graeme agreed, and headed off towards reception.

Steven fled to the cottage for the keys to the man-hole cover. He sprinted back up the hill, heaved the cover off, reached in to pull away the plug. He replaced the man-hole cover, washed his arm at the tap again and dashed to reception. He stuck his head round the door. "Hi, Mum! All right if I show Mr Curtis and Alexander round one of the new caravans?"

"Yes, love. I've given the key to Graeme."

"Great. Mum, where's the electric mains trip switch in those new thirty-two foot Atlas Dakotas?"

"In the double wardrobe love. Why?"

"Oh, I just didn't want to look stupid if they asked me."

He ran down to the back of Mrs Granny's house. There stood Mr Curtis, Alexander and Graeme. And Lucy. Lucy was smiling sweetly and saying, "So I was wondering if you had a book about wildlife in America, because I have to do a school project on endangered species in different countries."

"Well, we could look later," Mr Curtis began.

"I know you've got bears and snakes and racoons. We see them in American films on TV," Lucy continued.

"This afternoon, we'll ..." Mr Curtis tried again.

"And I know you've got skunks!" Lucy said triumphantly, wrinkling her pretty little nose, and smiling. "Do they really smell so bad?"

"You bet!" Alexander assured her. "Steven and me were just ..."

"Hello!" Steven interrupted loudly. "Mr Curtis, this is my friend Graeme."

"Yes, we've met this young man. Your sister introduced us. She was wanting to borrow a book ..."

"Thank you very much, Mr Curtis," Lucy said in her sweetest voice. "I'll come round for it later." She smiled, turned and skipped off towards the cottage.

"Lucy's amazing," Graeme whispered to Steven. "Her delaying tactics are cool!"

"So you're gonna show us one of the new caravans, are you, Steven?" Mr Curtis drawled.

"Yes. It's an Atlas Dakota. Graeme's family's got one, too."

"Your father's pleased with it, is he?"

"Yes," Graeme replied. "We all love it. My mum says it's home from home."

"Then lead on, young man," Mr Curtis said to Steven.

Graeme handed the key to Steven, and he opened both the caravan doors and showed everyone in. "We call this one the front door because it leads into the sitting-room. And this is the back door, because it's beside the kitchen. This sofa can be made into beds." Steven demonstrated. "But of course, there are two separate bedrooms. Here's the double one." All four of them trooped inside. "It has a nice roomy wardrobe," Steven said, opening the door and peering inside. "And lots of cupboard space." He showed them the shower room and the kitchen, then led them back into the sitting-room. "Of course, we've had a bit of trouble with the electrics over the winter." His heart began to thud. "It was the gales, you know, with the site being so high up."

"Can't your father fix it?" Jonathan Curtis asked sharply.

"Er, yes, of course. It's no problem to my dad. But this caravan isn't going to be occupied till next weekend, so he left it till last. He thought, if we get some strong winds this weekend, he could end up having to do the job twice."

"Yeah, I guess." Mr Curtis seemed satisfied.

Steven switched the light on, then off. "Seems all right now. There's a fridge, and this reading lamp, and the television's very good. Why don't you try it?" Steven began to edge towards the other end of the caravan. Graeme edged with him. "Tell you what. We'll just leave you to look round, and we'll come back later, to lock up." Steven had heard his dad say that to people who were thinking of buying a caravan.

"OK, son. We got you," Mr Curtis agreed.

Steven and Graeme headed towards the caravan's back door. Steven opened the shower door to obscure the view. Then he opened the back door and shut it again loudly. He pulled Graeme after him into the bigger bedroom, closed the door behind them, and crept inside the wardrobe. He and Graeme squatted down. A chink of daylight came through the crack of the door, just one centimetre open. Steven grinned at Graeme's astonished face. Then he removed the cover from the electric switch box, and waited. "This big switch is the mains," he whispered. "It controls the other switches." Graeme looked uncertain. "Don't worry. You can't get a shock. It's just an on/off switch."

They heard Alexander say, "Wonder what's on TV, Dad?"

"We haven't come to watch TV, son."

"I know. But Steven said to try it. I just wanted to see if it works." He switched on. Steven and Graeme heard him turn the volume up, then Steven switched off the electric power mains switch.

"Oh! What happened, Dad? I didn't touch anything."

Steven turned the power back on. He waited till he heard Alexander change channel, then he turned the mains switch off again.

"Maybe it's a problem with the power supply, like Steven said," Mr Curtis suggested.

"Try the light switch, Dad."

Steven heard a click, then he switched the mains on again.

"Well! Will you look at that! The light came on, but not when I switched it on!"

Steven repeated this several times, till he heard Alexander say, "Crumbs, Dad! It's like Christmas tree lights in here!"

Hot and cramped in the wardrobe, Steven and Graeme began to giggle silently. They heard Mr Curtis and Alexander trying every switch they could find, until finally, just as Steven felt he couldn't control his laughter any longer, he heard Mr Curtis say, "This is ridiculous! If they can get power up the Rocky Mountains, they can certainly get it up this pimple of a hill. I'll have a word with Alan MacGregor about it. See if he can't do his job a bit better than this!" Steven heard the caravan door slam, and the voices disappear into the distance. He didn't feel like laughing any more. They crept out of the wardrobe, and shut the bedroom and shower doors. Finally, Steven locked up the caravan and they headed back to reception.

"The Plan's not working, is it?" Graeme said thoughtfully.

"If he tells my dad, I'll *really* be for it." Steven pulled a face.

"Fooling Alexander is one thing. Taking his dad in is quite another," Graeme agreed.

"But the best bit's yet to come," Steven said, feeling brighter. "Whether it works or not, we're in for the best laugh yet!"

By late afternoon, Graeme had finished the fliers. Arriving at the back door of the cottage, he announced proudly, "I did enough for one for every caravan, and a few left over to put in reception."

"Better start giving them out now," Mum suggested, "Before it gets dusk. Just do the As and Bs because we know everyone in those. But miss out B11. Mr Jackson doesn't like to be disturbed."

So Steven, Graeme and Lucy took a handful each, and set off around the caravan site. "Pity caravans don't have letter boxes," Steven commented.

"Will we have to knock on every door, then?" Lucy asked. "It'll take ages."

"Yep. But people take more notice if you speak to them," Steven tried to reassure her.

It was a long job, but some people were interested and listened carefully.

At the fork leading to Hooper's Reach, Lucy asked, "Have we done B12 and 13?"

"Er, I think so. Er, dunno," Graeme replied. "The caravans all look the same."

"They don't!" Steven objected. "Look! That's an eight berth, but that ..." he pointed to another Dakota further up, "That's only a six berth."

"Oh. OK." Graeme didn't sound convinced.

"We need a system!" Lucy declared. "We need to write down all the numbers of the caravans. Then we should take the list with us, and tick off each caravan as we've done it."

"That's a good idea!" Steven agreed, his enthusiasm returning. "And we should tick if they're in. 'Cos if they're out, we can go back again tomorrow."

So they went back to the cottage and wrote a list of all the caravan numbers. But by the time they had finished, it was almost dark. Steven didn't mind the dark, but dinner was smelling good, and handing out fliers wasn't as exciting as playing tricks on Alexander and his father.

Chapter 8

Chills and Thrills

Easter Sunday dawned bright and sunny. Steven and Lucy hunted in the garden for Easter eggs, while Lucy sang, "Holiday Club's a-comin', Holiday Club's a-comin'." Then they all sat down to a big family breakfast. Mum had laid the table beautifully, with yellow napkins and a vase of daffodils. Steven felt full of Easter sunshine and anticipation.

Just as they were finishing breakfast, Graeme appeared. "My dad was wondering if Steven and Lucy would like to come out with us this afternoon," he announced.

"Great! Yes please!" Steven and Lucy said together.

"That's very kind of him," Steven's dad smiled. "It's a lovely day for an outing."

"Dad asked me where I thought you might like to go, so I said the Deer Park," Graeme said, looking hard at Steven.

"Or Moorlands Open Farm," Lucy suggested. "There'll be lambs and kids now, and …"

"The Deer Park would be just fine," Steven said firmly, looking hard at Lucy.

"Great. We'll pick you up at two o'clock," Graeme said, retreating.

"Say Happy Easter to your mum and dad for us," Steven's mum called after him.

Steven and Lucy went to visit Mrs Granny, who was very pale but smiling, and listening to Easter hymns on the radio. "Are you and your family going to church this morning, dear?" she asked Steven.

"Er, I think my dad's busy," he faltered. Mrs Granny had always told them Easter Sunday was the most important day of the year. And Steven believed it. But the season was about to begin ...

"Of course, dear," Mrs Granny went on, "And I'm sorry to be so useless at the moment!"

"You'll be better soon, Mrs Granny," Lucy said, "now that the summer's coming." Mrs Granny smiled then, though Steven thought it was a sad sort of smile.

Steven and Lucy spent the rest of the morning giving out fliers around the caravan site.

Steven, Lucy and Graeme had been to the Deer Park before, but there was always something new to see. They looked at several enclosures of different breeds of deer. Lucy had always loved the Kids' Korner, with pets that the children could hold. Steven was fascinated by the big cages for different sorts of owls. They saw the field of Highland cattle, with their strong horns and shaggy ginger hair. They passed the pond for ducks and geese, the tea shop, the adventure playground, and finally they arrived at the visitors' centre.

The real reason for wanting to go to the Deer Park had been Steven's idea. He wanted to see the video presentation again. He had watched it lots of times. He always loved it, but this time it was part of The Plan. He settled himself on the end of the line, while Mr and Mrs Robertson, Graeme and Lucy filed in to the video room to take a seat. As the lights went down, he quietly took a small battery-operated cassette tape recorder from his rucksack. He placed it carefully on his lap, and waited for the video to begin. The photography was of the Highlands and the west coast in all the different seasons.

"The great Caledonian Pine Forest used to cover most of Scotland," the voice on the video informed them. "Now, only scattered remnants of the mighty forest remain, but these woods provide a safe haven for many of Scotland's wild animals."

On the wide screen, they watched a harsh sweep of majestic winter landscape, the Scots pines heavy with snow.

"It's not difficult, on a dark winter's day," the video voice continued, "To imagine wolves, bears and lynx still roaming the forest, searching for prey." Chill shivers of delight ran down Steven's spine as the plaintive howling of wolves and yowling of wildcats filled the hall. He pressed 'record' on his cassette machine, and held his finger over the pause button.

As the voice returned, he paused the tape. "It's two hundred and fifty years since the last wolf was shot in Britain, and three hundred and fifty since noblemen hunted wild boar. But on windy days, the forest itself mimics their call."

Steven lifted the pause button, and the sound of wind in the pines, first sighing and moaning, then whistling and keening filled the darkened room.

"Red squirrels arrived in Scotland at the end of the last ice age, at the same time as the Scots pine," the voice continued, and Steven watched again the antics of the red squirrel. He heard again about the dangers of the grey squirrel. He felt heart-broken again that stalkers and sportsmen had to shoot red deer every season, because there were too many of them, and they were destroying the trees.

Towards the end of the presentation Steven remembered there was some information about birds. Barn owls and tawny owls could often be seen in Scotland. There was the funny capercaillie, looking like a turkey, and of course, the majestic golden eagle. But at the very end, as the viewers watched areas of meadow and farmland, came the brittle, tuneless call of the corncrake. Steven captured the rasping sound on tape, and remembered how his mum had once said, "Someone should tell him to leave the choir."

Steven put the tape recorder away in his bag before the lights went up, hoping that the little built-in microphone had done its job.

Back at the caravan site, the warm sunny weather had tempted everyone out to walk in the hills, or to saunter along the beach. It seemed no-one was sitting around in their caravans. Dad was at reception. Steven and Graeme took a few fliers and Steven asked his dad to give them to anyone who dropped in. "And here's the petition, Dad," Steven reminded him. "Please get everyone to sign. Tell them it's very important."

"Why don't you stick around for a while and tell them yourself, son," Dad suggested. "It'd carry more weight, coming from you."

"Well, er, we've got things to do," Steven said mysteriously. "Anyway, it's a nice day. Too nice to be stuck indoors."

"OK, son. Lucky for some," Dad said, but he had a twinkle in his eye.

"Great! Thanks, Dad!"

"Thanks, Mr MacGregor," Graeme added, and they shot out of reception and towards the store. Mum was at home, puzzling over the accounts books, spread out all over the kitchen table, and Lucy got out her sketch book to draw red deer. So there was no one to raise an eyebrow as Steven and Graeme carried reels of electric cable, extension leads, adaptors and light bulbs up to the Reach, unrolling cable from the reel as they went. They plugged it into the highest empty touring placement which had a power supply.

"Are you sure you know what you're doing?" Graeme asked.

"Don't worry," Steven reassured him. "I've been doing electrics with my dad since I was nine. He's taught me all the correct safety procedures."

Although Steven knew that anyone on the site was free to walk up there and enjoy the views, he was relying on the fact that people seldom did. They walked downhill, instead, along the lane, or into the village. Or they took their cars to the coast. So there was no-one there to watch Steven climb as high as he could into a beech tree on the left of the clearing, while Graeme held the cable up to him. He had attached a light bulb to the end in the tree. Then he repeated the operation, in a tree on the other side of the clearing. At last the job was finished, and Graeme crept under the bush to the junction where the on/off switch was, while Steven stood by the fence to admire his handiwork.

"OK," he called quietly. "On!"

Graeme switched on.

"Rats! It's no good. In darkness, the light will be too white, and if I move like this …" he stepped sideways, "… I can see the light bulb."

Graeme switched off and came out of hiding. "How about some green tissue paper? You got any in the cottage?"

"Nae. But Lucy might. Trouble is, I wasn't going to let her in on this."

"She'll be OK with it," Graeme assured him. "Anyway, we're going to need someone else to do the switches. I can't do lights and sound."

"OK. Maybe," Steven agreed reluctantly.

In the cottage, Lucy was sitting at the table drawing. As usual. Mum was still cooking, so Steven beckoned Lucy outside. "Got any green tissue paper?" he asked.

"What for?"

"To make ghostly lights for a haunted forest."

"Aye, right!" said Lucy with a scornful toss of her ginger pony tail. She turned to go back inside.

"Tell her properly," Graeme urged. "Explain it all." Lucy half turned.

"OK," Steven agreed slowly. "Lucy, get your jacket. You can come in on The Plan with us." Lucy paused, and looked at their eager faces. Then she grabbed her jacket from the hook by the door.

The three walked along the empty lane. "Thing is," Steven began, "we're trying to get at Jonathan Curtis through Alexander. Trying to persuade him that it's not a good idea to put caravans on the Reach."

"He listens to Alexander," Graeme added.

"And *I* can get Alexander to listen to me!" Steven finished.

"So what's with the green tissue paper?" Lucy asked.

"We're going to tell Alexander that the Reach is haunted and that wolves return when the full moon falls on Easter day," Steven grinned.

"Cool!" said Lucy, her eyes shining. "Are we going to wear sheets and moan 'Whooo' …?"

"Don't be daft. The ghosts are going to be the wolves that used to live in the Great Caledonian Pine Forest."

"So we'll borrow someone's dog, and dress *him* in a sheet?" Lucy was doubtful.

"No," Steven said, trying to be patient. "I've recorded the wolf howls and wildcat calls off the Deer Park video. We'll switch eerie lights on, and play the tape in the distance. We'll put Alexander off so much that he'll persuade his dad to pack up and leave!"

"Cool!" Lucy squeaked again. "What do I have to do?"

"You have to pretend to be too frightened to stay up there, and run off home …"

"Not likely! He'll think I'm a wimp!"

"But what you'll actually do," Steven went on quickly, "is to creep behind the bushes and switch the lights on and off. That way, you'll be able to share the fun when he gets scared."

"Yeah!" Lucy agreed enthusiastically.

"But first," Graeme reminded them, "we need some green tissue paper."

"Mum's got a green shower cap," Lucy suggested.

"Yes! We could put it over the light bulb. The light wouldn't be on long enough to burn it," Graeme agreed.

"And Jemima's got a purple sequinned dress with a net petticoat," she continued.

"Who's Jemima?"

"Her best doll," Steven said in disgust.

So the three of them went up to Hooper's Reach again, and wrapped a green shower cap round one light bulb, and a purple frilly doll's dress round the other. Lucy squeaked with delight when Steven switched both the lights on, and Graeme turned on the tape and tested the volume. Up, down. Up, down. It finished with the corncrake's scratchy call.

"Yeah! That's brilliant!" Lucy grinned. "It nearly scared *me*, and it's not even dark yet!"

"How're we going to get Alexander up here?" Graeme asked suddenly.

"I've got that all figured out," Steven assured him. "You got your bike here?"

"Yes. It's still on the bike rack on the back of the car."

"Good. Well, after supper, when it's just getting dark, we'll call for Alexander, and ask if he wants to come out. He's sure to say yes, because he likes showing off his posh bike."

So as they walked back down the path, Steven outlined the final stage of The Plan to Graeme and Lucy. As they reached the cottage, Dad was at the back door. "How did the fliers go, Dad?" Steven asked.

"How many people signed the petition?" Lucy added.

"Well, everyone who read the flier said how good it was," Dad began. Graeme beamed, and Steven clapped him on the back.

"But how many people signed, Mr McGregor?" Graeme insisted.

"Er, about half a dozen," Dad admitted.

"Six! That's not enough!" Lucy wailed.

"It's a start," Dad said. "And the holiday's only just beginning. We've got lots more time. Some of the people were new, and didn't really know what we were on about. Some were in a hurry, and said they'd read it carefully later. No-one refused."

"That's the trouble. People don't care," Steven grumbled.

"Well, it's your job to make them care, son," Dad said gently.

"I'm trying, Dad," Steven said mournfully. "But we're not finished yet!" he said more cheerfully.

Chapter 9

The Plan

Mum had cooked a magnificent dinner of roast chicken, crispy potatoes and vegetables, and Dad had produced his speciality, hot chocolate pudding and ice cream. Before they'd cleared the table, Graeme appeared, riding round and round on his bike in the lane.

Steven got his bike out, and they went to ring on Mrs Granny's doorbell. Mrs Curtis came to the door with a bright smile and a warm welcome.

"Hello honey!" she beamed.

"Er, hello, Mrs Curtis. We were wondering whether Alexander would like to come out on his bike with us."

"I'm sure he would, honey. I'll call him. It would be swell for you two to be good pals. It's just so lucky for him to have you living so close. Say, do you play baseball?" Steven shook his head. "We'd love to teach you sometime. Alexander's a good pitcher and I can backstop." She went inside. Steven's conscience tweaked a little. How could a man as horrible as Jonathan Curtis have such a nice wife? But it's all in a good cause, he told himself. Anyway, nature was on his side. The evening was dry and clear, and the moon was full.

The boys rode along the lane three abreast,

because there was no traffic at all. They talked about bikes, soccer and animals.

"Yes," said Steven finally, trying to keep his voice serious. "You've certainly got lots of animals in the States. What you haven't got, is history."

"What d'you mean?

"Well, there used to be wolves here two hundred and fifty years ago, and wild boar a hundred years before that. America was hardly discovered by then. At least, there wasn't anyone around to write about the wildlife."

"Maybe it was the same as now," Alexander ventured.

"Maybe. But we don't know that, do we? I mean, Scotland used to be covered by the Great Caledonian Pine Forest, and there used to be elks and lynx. Now we've just got the Scottish wildcat. We've got to look after what we've got. There's some talk of scientists bringing wolves back to Scotland."

"Hey, Steve!" Graeme interrupted, exactly as planned. "Remember that old story? The one about wolves?"

"What, that one about Easter Sunday night?"

"Yeah. About wolf spooks."

"You don't believe that stuff, do you?" Steven asked scornfully.

"No, of course not," Graeme laughed. "It just made me think, with the full moon an' all."

"What story? What wolves?" Alexander asked, his eyes bright.

"Och, it's just an old wives' tale," Steven said.

"But if it's a Scottish history old wives' tale, you'd better tell me!"

Steven yawned and tried to look bored, but inside

he was laughing with delight. He had succeeded in arousing Alexander's interest. Full score for round one of The Plan.

"Well," Graeme began, pretending to be unwilling. "the story says that the ancient wolves can be heard in the parts of the Caledonian forest which are still left ..."

"If it's a full moon ..." Steven interrupted.

"And if it's Easter Sunday night!" Graeme finished.

"And it is!" Alexander declared. "Both of those!"

"And the top of Mrs Granny's land is part of the Caledonian pine forest," Steven added for extra effect.

"Let's go up there, just to prove it's not true," Graeme suggested.

"Nae. I've been out all day. I'm tired," said Steven, yawning.

"If you won't go, people will think you're chicken!" Graeme challenged.

"Me? Chicken? On yer bike!" Steven laughed. "OK. You never know, there might be people walking up there. We could try howling, to scare them." He tried an unrealistic wolf howl.

"I don't think you'd fool anyone," Alexander told him.

"Oh well," Steven grinned. "Let's leave our bikes and walk up there." They cycled in at Steven's gate and Lucy came outside, as if by chance. "Wanna come up to the Reach? We're gonna look for ghost wolves."

"What? That old story? You don't believe that stuff, do you?"

"Course not. We're just going for a laugh,"

Graeme assured her.

"Or are you too scared?" Steven challenged.

"Who, me? Not likely! I'm coming." She grabbed her jacket.

"What have they been telling you, Alexander?" she asked on the way up.

"Oh, just about the ghost wolves coming back if it's Easter Sunday and there's a full moon."

"Did they tell you it had to be part of the Caledonian pine forest?" Lucy asked.

"Yeah, yeah. And that Aunt Rhoda's land is part of the forest," Alexander added.

"You know why it's called Hooper's Reach, don't you?" Graeme asked suddenly. Steven looked at him sharply. This bit wasn't in The Plan. Graeme continued, "It used to be called Lupus Reach, but over the centuries the name got changed. Lupus is Latin for wolf. The wolves reached as far as here. Lupus Reach!" He looked round at them triumphantly.

Steven was longing to ask, "How do you know?" It sounded very convincing. His scalp prickled with anticipation, but he didn't ask. He just raised his eyebrows and forced a smile, first at Graeme, and then at Lucy. He tried to make his eyes say, "Let's stick to what we agreed!"

Lucy seemed to understand. "Hey, Steve! It really is a full moon!" She pretended she'd only just noticed.

"Wow! You are scared, after all," Steven teased.

"N-no, I'm not," said Lucy. But she made her voice sound wobbly.

"Never mind, Lucy." Graeme said his carefully rehearsed lines. "If there *are* any wolves, they'll stay deep in the forest. They won't come to the edge, where we are."

"But wolves used to come right into people's camps, to get food," Steven told them. "And if they couldn't find an ox cooking over a camp fire, they used to take a child instead."

Graeme began to drag his feet, and Lucy to shuffle a bit.

"Come on, you two," Alexander said, but a bit less certainly now. "It's not really true."

"Mind you, they say there's no smoke without fire," Steven muttered. "There must be some truth in the stories, or how would they have lasted so long?"

They reached the high ground, and Steven leaned on the fence and looked out at the sea sparkling in the moonlight. Lucy was facing the other way. "Look, Lucy. It's a lovely view."

"I'm not turning my back on the woods," Lucy whimpered. "Whatever it is, I want to see it coming." She leaned her back on the fence, and stared with big eyes into the blackness. "What was that?" she gasped, grabbing Steven's arm.

"What? Where?" he hissed.

"That noise! Rustling! Over there!" She pointed, and started to cry.

"Well, go home then if you're scared. We don't want any waterworks!" he mocked. Lucy ran away.

In the silence which followed, Steven felt his mouth corners twitch. He wanted to laugh. Lucy was a brilliant actress.

"Huh! Girls!" said Graeme in disgust. "Well, it doesn't bother me!" And he marched a few paces towards the trees and looked round. Suddenly, he gasped.

"What?" said Alexander, in a voice which was higher than usual. "What is it?"

"Nothing. It was nothing," Graeme said, breathing heavily. Then he stepped back suddenly.

"Crumbs! What's the matter," Steven demanded, stepping towards him.

"I thought I saw something. Up there." Graeme pointed into a tree. "Yes. There! Look!"

Alexander came up to stand beside them. High up in the tree, an eerie green light glowed. Then disappeared. Then reappeared. Alexander gasped. "What is it?" he whispered hoarsely, looking all around.

"Look! What's that?" Graeme pointed the other way, and the three of them saw a dim purple glow, which came and went like the green one.

"Hey, don't you think we ought to be going?" Graeme asked shakily.

"No! You're just scared," Steven mocked.

"No I'm not!" Graeme said, but a moment later, he made a big show of looking at his watch. "Look, it's getting late. I promised to get back to the caravan. I'll get a row if I stay out any longer. Bye. See you tomorrow." He ran off down the lane.

"What a pair of wimps," Steven said loudly, as if he was trying to bolster up his own courage. "Just think how we can tease them in the morning!" He laughed very deliberately, then became quiet, and listened. He tilted his head.

"What! Did you hear something?" Alexander said, standing close.

"No. Or if I did, it was the wind."

"There isn't any wind," Alexander whispered.

They listened again. This time it was definitely

there: a distant, mournful, howling, growing gradually louder.

"It's them! It's the wolves! It must be," Alexander whimpered. "Nothing else sounds like that!"

Steven turned to him, putting on the most terrified face he could manage. "I never told you!" he squeaked.

"What?"

"The end of the story!"

"What! What!"

"If you *really* hear the wolves, you either disappear without trace, or people never believe you, and it drives you slowly mad, so that within a year you're dribbling and wetting yourself!"

Alexander's chin trembled, and tears welled up in his eyes.

"We've only got one chance," Steven said, with a convincing wobble in his voice.

"What?"

"Stare them out! Beat them at their own game! Don't show you're scared! Show them we can stay here longer than they can!"

"But ..."

"Keep your eyes wide open, and look over there," he pointed. "Let's stand back to back. I'll look over here."

So with the howling of wolves in his ears, and his teeth chattering with fear, Alexander planted his feet firmly and stared. Behind him, Steven crept silently to his bird-watching hide, and disappeared inside it.

The howling was so near now, the wolves could have been behind the next tree.

"Steve!" Alexander whispered.

Silence.

"Steven!" he hissed again.

More silence.

"Steven, they're getting nearer. It's not working," Alexander whimpered, looking round.

"Steven! Where are you?" Alexander turned round in a circle, first one way, then the other. All alone, he let out a heart-rending wail, and ran off down the path, his howls interrupted by terrified sobs as his feet struck the ground, just as the rasping hoarse voice of the corncrake called out across the clearing.

Steven came out of his hide. The lights went off, and the wolves and the corncrake stopped. In the deepest part of Steven, a giggle began. Like a spring of fresh water in the depths of the earth, it rose up and up, till it lodged in his throat, almost choking him. Lucy appeared from behind the bushes where the extension lead was hidden. Graeme came from the other side, clutching the tape recorder. Steven's laughter burst out in a huge, roaring guffaw. He sank to his knees and hugged his belly, gasping for breath. The other two were just as bad. Lucy was shrieking with laughter, while Graeme tried to put his hand over her mouth, shaking and snorting. They sat in a triangle, rocking and giggling, until at last they were able to speak.

"Lucy, you were brilliant!" Graeme told her.

"You, too, Graeme. Seriously convincing!" Steven admired. "You've both got a future on the stage!"

"But the best bit," Lucy hiccuped, giggling uncontrollably again for a moment, "was the bit about dribbling and wetting yourself!" And all three of them rolled over and over on the mossy ground, enjoying it all again.

"That bit about Lupus Reach," Steven asked Graeme suddenly, remembering, "Is it true? How did you know?"

"Naw! I made it up on the spur of the moment. It just came into my mind! Anyway, who *was* Hooper?"

"Dunno. Have to ask Dad. Or Mrs Granny. Alexander said one of his relatives was called Mrs Hooper."

"Come on. We'd better get this stuff back to Dad's store," said Steven, getting up. "If he finds these cables and adaptors have gone, he'll have my guts for garters!" So he climbed the trees again, and unhooked the light bulb with the shower cap, and the one with the purple doll's dress. Lucy and Graeme wound up the cable, unplugged it from the touring site power point and put the equipment away in Steven's dad's store.

Chapter 10

Back to Square One

"There you are, you two! Just look at the time!" Mum exploded. "Wherever have you been?"

"Sorry, Mum," Lucy said. "We were only up at the Reach."

"At this time in the evening? Whatever were you doing?" Dad demanded.

"It's a lovely evening, Dad. The moon's bright. We could see clearly," Steven said, trying not to smile, despite his dad's angry frown.

"Well, you'd better have a quick glass of milk, and straight to bed, both of you," Mum declared, reaching two glasses down from the cupboard.

"And after supper tomorrow, you can stay in!" Dad announced.

They were only half way through their milk when there was a loud rap at the back door. It was Jonathan Curtis.

"So there you are, young man!" he shouted at Steven, stepping into the kitchen without being invited.

"Now what's all this about?" Dad asked, standing up.

"What's it about?" Mr Curtis repeated. "I'll tell you what it's about!" He was so angry, his chest was puffed out, and he was almost spitting. "It seems that this boy, here …" He poked his chin in

Steven's direction, "… has been telling my boy tall stories. Stories? No! Lies! Lies enough to terrify the living daylights out of him!"

Mr Curtis's face was as red as a tomato, and his eyes were blazing. He pushed his fair hair back and paced up and down the small kitchen. He seemed to fill the room. Lucy got up and stood behind Mum.

"What's all this?" Dad asked again. "What have you been saying, Steven?"

"Ridiculous lies, from beginning to end," Mr Curtis continued, not giving Steven chance to answer. "Three on to one. Ganging up on him with unkind pranks. Premeditated, it was! All worked out beforehand to scare the wits out of him!" He brought his fist down on the table in front of Steven. Steven jumped. The glass of milk shook. "*And* all this rubbish about difficulties with the power and plumbing to the high caravans, making out that your father can't even do his job properly. I suspect that was fairy tales, too. What sort of welcome to his home country was that, for my boy? And he thought you wanted to be friends with him!"

Steven felt his dad's eyes boring into him. He was deeply ashamed. And he was scared.

"Is this true, Steven?" Dad asked quietly.

How could he explain everything with one little word, yes or no? Steven stared into his milk.

"Look at me, Steven. Is this true?"

Steven looked at his dad. "Well, um, yes, but …"

"Dad!" Lucy exclaimed, "It wasn't like that! It was because we wanted to …"

"Lucy! Was it your idea?"

"No! Yes! Well, we ..."

Dad sighed. "Steven, was it your idea or Lucy's?"

"Mine."

"Lucy, you go up to bed. I'll come and speak to you later."

"But Dad! It's not fair! It wasn't like that!"

"Lucy!" Dad said, in his special serious voice. Lucy stopped speaking and rushed upstairs. They heard her sobbing as she went. Mum followed, and shut the door firmly behind her.

"Steven, is this true? Did you tell lies to frighten Alexander?"

"Yes, but we did it to show him."

"Show him what?"

"To show him that what they want to do is all wrong. No one will listen!" Hot tears of rage pricked the back of Steven's eyes and a heavy lump lodged in his throat. He couldn't look at Mr Curtis.

"It seems to me, Mr Curtis, that my son and I have some catching up to do. So I'd be grateful if you'd let us do that just now, and I'll come round and speak to you in the morning."

"You see that you do!" Mr Curtis stormed. "If I thought he was getting off scot free with this, this ..." He was so angry, he couldn't find his words. "This running around wild, terrorising the neighbourhood ..."

"I give you my word that we'll get to the bottom of this, and we'll do it fairly," Dad said, moving to the back door and opening it for Mr Curtis. "Good night."

When the door was closed again, the hot tears spilled out into Steven's milk. "I'm sorry Dad," he sobbed. "I never said you couldn't do your job properly. But I sort of promised Mrs Granny that I'd never let anyone put caravans on the Reach. We've worked all these years to make the site friendly to wildlife, then *he* has to come and spoil it all!"

Dad sat and listened quietly without interrupting.

"I know you work for Mrs Granny, so you have to do what she says. And I know the Curtises are related to her, and we're not. Well, not really. She wouldn't let them do it if she was well, would she?"

Dad shook his head sadly.

"What's the matter with her, Dad? Why doesn't she get better?"

"I don't know, son. She's been taking antibiotics almost all winter. I think she should see a specialist."

"She was talking about heaven, Dad. Do you think she's going to die?"

"I sincerely hope not, son." Dad seemed shocked. "I'll tell Mum to visit her in the morning, and persuade her to make an appointment ..."

"It's all happening too quick, Dad. I had to do what I could think of." So Steven told his dad about the three tricks he'd played on Alexander, and how he'd involved Lucy and Graeme. He explained about thinking Mr Curtis might listen to Alexander, but not to Steven himself. He even admitted the fight.

"People agree with us, Dad. See how they've been signing the petition in reception?"

"Aye, but not enough of them," his father added. "Nothing's been agreed, son. There's been so much work this week, with the season opening, and the good weather. And what with Mrs Granny being too poorly to take her usual share of the work, I didn't see the development thing as being so urgent. I agree that everything's happened very quickly. It seems a bit fishy that the Curtises have arrived just now. When I've got time, I'll ..."

"But Dad! There *isn't* any time."

"Aye, son. I'm beginning to see that." He ruffled Steven's hair affectionately.

They sat quietly for a while, then Dad said, "I think we both have some apologising to do. For a start, I'm sorry I didn't take the time to listen and talk to you about it. But in the morning, we'll both go round to Mrs Granny's and say sorry to the Curtises, and especially to Alexander. OK?"

"OK, Dad."

"You've got bags of energy, son, and you want to be independent. Your heart's in the right place, but some decisions are too big for you, and this is one of them. You always think you can do everything yourself, but you have to leave some things to the grown-ups. However, since you've got such a creative imagination, maybe you could put it to good use and think how to make that wee lad feel at home here."

"He's not a wee lad, Dad! He's bigger than me!"

"I expect he didn't feel big enough this evening!"

Steven chuckled, in spite of everything. "Actually, Dad, I reckon he lasted pretty well before he caved in and ran off. Longer than I think I would've!"

"Well, there you are then. Maybe he's not all bad."

"Dad? Who was Hooper? Why did he have the Reach named after him?"

"I don't know, son. I expect Mrs Granny knows. We'll ask her tomorrow."

"Alexander said his great-grandma was called Mrs Hooper."

Dad turned and looked hard at Steven. "Oh, she was, was she? I think I begin to smell a rat!"

"I can't smell anything!" Steven grinned.

"I'll definitely have to look into the Curtis family tree!" But instead, he made cups of drinking chocolate and got the biscuit tin out, and they laughed about light bulbs with green shower caps and purple doll's petticoats.

Steven was completely exhausted, but his mind was so full, he thought he would never sleep. In the end, he didn't even remember climbing into bed.

Chapter 11

The Giant Killer

Steven slept late on Monday morning. When he finally woke up, he wanted to stay in bed. He wasn't looking forward to making his apology.

As he lay staring at his bedroom ceiling, Lucy put her head round the door. Her green eyes were big and solemn. She came in and sat on the end of his bed. "Get up, lazybones! Mrs Granny's gone into hospital, and you're coming with me to help at the Holiday Club."

"What?" Steven sat up and rubbed his eyes. His head felt too big, and his teeth were furry.

"Mrs Granny was so ill in the night, Mrs Curtis got worried and sent for the doctor. And the doctor sent her into hospital."

"Is she going to be all right?"

"I don't know. Mum's gone to see her and take her some things. Toothbrush and stuff."

They sat in solemn silence for a moment, and Steven tried to gather his thoughts. Then he said, "What did you say about the Holiday Club?"

"Dad says you've got to come."

"But it's for little kids."

"No it's not. I'm going."

"Yes, but you'll be the oldest one there. You and a couple of girls from your class."

"But you've got to go and be a helper. The

minister phoned. They need a boy. The helpers for the younger group are all girls."

Steven groaned. "All girls. I'm not going."

"You've got to, silly."

"I've got a headache." Steven snuggled down into his bed again.

"Come on, slow coach. We've got to leave soon." Lucy went out. Mr Curtis's words came back to Steven, "Terrorising the neighbourhood." Maybe Dad wanted to keep him out of the way. Just in case. Steven felt let down.

Downstairs, Dad was washing the breakfast dishes. "Come on, son. It's all go today. Did Lucy tell you about Mrs Granny?"

"Yeah. Is she going to be all right, Dad?"

"I hope so. If you ask me, it's the best place for her. She should have been in hospital weeks ago."

"Dad, can't I stay and help you this morning? I could stay in reception. I could ask people to sign the petition. I wouldn't do anything … you know … anything silly."

"Rosie's going to do reception today. Mum'll be back from the hospital soon, but I've got to go up to Inverness. There's a couple of caravans there that might be a real bargain. I'll have to stay overnight, but I'll be back by tea time tomorrow. I'll phone if there's any change of plan."

"But Dad! You were going to come with me to say sorry to the Curtises!"

"That household's at sixes and sevens this morning. They were up most of the night with Mrs Granny. We'll go tomorrow. Put that bag in the van for me, would you, son?" Steven took the van keys from the hook in the kitchen and picked up

Dad's overnight bag. Dad followed him with a map, a file and a pile of papers. "Brr! Not as warm as it looks. Think I'll wear my thicker jacket." He went back into the house and changed jackets.

"Don't worry, son," he said finally. But it didn't help. Steven was worried.

There were about forty children at the Holiday Club in the village hall. Steven liked Mr and Mrs McKenzie, the friendly, smiley couple who ran it. Lucy went to join a group doing crafts. Mrs McKenzie was at one end of the hall rehearsing a play with some children.

"Good on you for coming, Steven," Mr McKenzie said, slapping him on the back. "Now these youngsters have opted for football." About a dozen eager five-and six-year-olds gathered around them. There was one little girl among them.

An older girl, about Steven's age, suddenly bounded up, wearing a Celtic strip, and smiling. "Amanda," Mr McKenzie continued, "Steven's come to help you with the football. Perhaps the two of you could take this lot on to the field at the back for half an hour. Here's my whistle."

"Thanks Mr McKenzie," the girl said. He nodded and went back into the hall. "Wow! Thanks for coming, Steven." She smiled even more. "I'm hopeless at football!" The two of them and the younger children spilled out on to the grass.

Steven looked at the girl. She must be the same age as him, maybe just a bit older. Her blue eyes shone, and her blond hair shone to match. She was vaguely familiar. Steven didn't know why his face felt suddenly warm.

"Amanda. Have you forgotten?" She read his thoughts. "I used to be in Mrs Granderton's Sunday school class at the same time as you! Remember when we did a Christmas nativity play, and you were Joseph and I was Mary?"

How could he have forgotten? Her smile was dazzling.

"Oh, yeah. But you used to …"

"I know. I haven't been around much because I used to go to boarding school because my dad's in the army, and he kept getting moved around. But my parents have split up now, and my mum's got a job here. I'll be going to the High School in August."

"Uh, me too," said Steven.

The little boys were surprisingly good at football, and the little girl was the best of the lot. Amanda, far from being hopeless, was brilliant, both with the children and with the ball. Steven put them through their paces, remembering the warm-up exercises and skills practices he'd been taught at school. He enjoyed himself. By the end of the session, his headache was gone, and he felt fresh and alive. Yesterday was a distant memory.

It was lunch time. The children sat at folding tables to eat their packed lunches. Mum had made some hasty cheese rolls for Steven and Lucy, and put in crisps and apples at the last minute.

While they were eating, Amanda said, "Why don't you come to STEP?"

"What's that?"

"St Thomas's Eleven Plus. It's a club for overelevens. Lots of Mrs Granderton's old Sunday school class go now."

"What do you do?"

"Oh, games, quizzes, Bible discussions, weekend camps, orienteering, swimming outings, pizza-making competitions... And we laugh a lot." She was laughing already.

"Well, er, I might."

During story time, the children sat on a carpet, but Steven, feeling grown up, sat with the leaders and helpers on a row of chairs at the back. The story was about David, the young Jewish shepherd boy, who killed the giant, Goliath. Steven knew the story well from Mrs Granny's Sunday School class, but it was clear that many of the children hadn't heard it before. Mr McKenzie was a wonderful story-teller, and the children listened, spellbound. He had funny cartoon pictures on an overhead projector.

He told how the whole army of Israel was frightened of Goliath, because he was so big and fierce. But David told Saul, the king of Israel, that he wasn't afraid. God had helped him protect his sheep from lions and bears, so this giant Philistine soldier was no problem.

David chose five smooth stones from the stream. The children held their breath as David put a stone into his sling and stood in front of the giant. Goliath laughed at him because he was young and small. David wasn't put off. He whirled the sling round his head a couple of times, took aim, and let the stone fly. It hit the giant right in the middle of his forehead, and he went crashing down, armour and all. The Philistine army ran away.

The army of Israel cheered. The children cheered, too.

"So you see, children," Mr MacKenzie finished, "You don't have to be big and grown up. David knew he couldn't do the job alone. But he wasn't alone. God was with him. God helps young people, if they trust him. And then, how different everything can be!"

Next, Mrs MacKenzie's drama group acted out the story. Some small children were David's flock, wearing the sheep masks they had made earlier. The boy who played the part of David put on the heavy armour that King Saul wanted to lend him. Lucy had made the armour out of foil cartons. Goliath was one of the helpers, who crashed to the ground so dramatically that one of the smallest children got frightened.

At the end of the drama, Mr MacKenzie invited Amanda to the front. "Now Amanda's going to tell us her story," he told the children. He turned to Amanda. "How old are you, Amanda?"

"I'm twelve now," she told them, and continued, "but last year, when I was eleven, everything changed for me. For a start, my mum and dad split up, which meant I stopped going to boarding school, and came to live here with my mum and my sister. But something even more important happened. You see, I think I used to be a bit like one of those Israelite soldiers, you know, the ones who just watched, but who were too scared to fight Goliath themselves. The Israelites were God's chosen people, but they didn't really trust him for themselves. They must have known a lot about God. Like me. I'd been going to

Sunday School for years. I knew all the Bible stories. But I had never really trusted God for myself. I suddenly realised the difference. I mean, between David and the rest. And I wanted to be like David. He acted like God was his friend. So I asked God to be my friend. I told him I was going to trust him. And he's helped me so much, over my parents splitting up, and the move, and going to a new school, and making new friends and everything."

Amanda's eyes sparkled as she told her story, but Steven knew it was taking some courage to do it. Her neck was going red, and the blush worked its way up to her cheeks. Steven reckoned she was as brave as David.

Mr MacKenzie thanked her, and announced a song. Several of the helpers picked up guitars, one stood at the keyboard, and another played the drums. First they played an action song for the smaller children. Steven knew it well:

"He made the stars to shine
He made the rolling sea ..."

The children flexed their fingers for twinkling stars, and rolled their arms for the waves. Amanda stood at the front, showing the new kids how to do it. Steven remembered how he used to hate the song. He and his ten-year-old friends had thought it was babyish.

"He made the mountains high
And he made me ..."

They used to exaggerate the actions leaping up to indicate how high the mountains were, and beating their chests for "meeeeeeee."

"And this is why I love him,
  For me he bled and died,
  The God of all creation
  Became the crucified."

Thinking about the words now, after what Amanda had said, Steven felt ashamed when he recalled how they used to fling their arms wide for the shape of a cross, deliberately biffing each other on the head, then giggling about it. He felt worse when he thought again about how *he* had spent Easter Sunday, the most important day of the year.

As they were leaving, Mr MacKenzie said to Steven, "Thanks again for helping, lad. Come again if you'd like to."

"Thanks. I've enjoyed it. I've got a friend who might like to come. And there's another boy, too ..."

"Yes of course! Bring them along. The more, the merrier!"

When Steven and Lucy arrived home for tea, Dad was away in Inverness, and Mum had taken over from Rosie in reception. Steven took the key from its hiding place behind the plant pot, and unlocked the back door. They flung down their bags and poured drinks of juice from the fridge. Steven took his drink to the window. He gasped.

"What?" Lucy demanded, joining him.

An enormous JCB earth mover was parked at the bottom of the site. Next to it, just behind the bushes, was a scruffy old two-sleeper caravan. A group of children stood admiringly around the JCB.

Ever since Dad had argued with Mr Curtis, a little cold ball of fear had lain heavily in Steven's heart. Now it stretched out Jack Frost fingers into his throat and along his arms and legs. "I dread to think what *that* thing's doing here," he said, shuddering.

"Let's go and ask Mum about it," Lucy suggested. They ran out, and paused to take a closer look at the huge vehicle. The small children who stood around were exclaiming about it.

"Wow!"

"Cool!"

"I'm going to drive one of those when I'm big!"

Steven and Lucy burst into reception. "Mum! What's that earth mover for?"

Mum looked up from the accounts she was puzzling over. "Moving earth, I expect, love."

"Mum!" Steven groaned, exasperated. "Which earth? Earth from where? And why?"

"Sorry, love. I wasn't concentrating." She closed the book and smiled, ready to pay attention.

Lucy tried this time. "Mum! There's an enormous JCB parked at the bottom of the site. Are they going to dig up the top ground?"

"I've not heard anything about it, love. I'm sure Dad's got it all under control."

"But Dad's not here!"

"He'll be back tomorrow. Maybe he's planning to prune some trees over on the far side."

"But Mum!" Steven objected. "He usually uses the van and the trailer to take the branches away. This thing's gigantic!"

"Well, let's go over and look," Mum said, gathering an armful of papers. "It's time I went home and made us some tea, anyway."

She locked the door to reception, and they walked over to the cottage, stopping at the JCB on the way. Steven looked up at it. The shovel was immense. You could fit a person in there, he thought. Six people, in fact!

"Do you think the workmen are in that little caravan?" he asked.

"Probably, love. We could knock on the door and ask them about it. Let me just go and dump these papers."

As they went into the cottage, the phone was ringing. "It might be Dad," Mum said, grabbing it. Steven and Lucy waited, hopping from foot to foot with impatience. Finally Mum put the phone down and turned towards them. "It was Mrs Curtis. She's just going into the hospital to visit Mrs Granny. She must realise I haven't got any transport, with Dad away. She offered me a lift, so I accepted."

Steven's heart sank.

"I won't be away very long, pets. I ought to go. It's been a hard time for Anne-Marie. She told me earlier that Jonathan's quite discouraged. She says he's planning to leave if he can't make a success of a business project here. Pity, really. They were so keen to settle in Scotland. Make yourselves a sandwich. I'll bring chips from the village when I come back. I'm going to tell the Robertsons where

I'm off to. I expect Mrs Robertson will be down here in a minute." She blew a kiss to each of them, grabbed her handbag, and left.

Steven flopped down on a kitchen chair. He felt tired suddenly, and hungry, and very fed up. "I'm going to phone Dad," he declared. "I don't know why he didn't tell us anything about the plans." He went over to the phone on the kitchen wall and dialled Dad's mobile number.

After a moment, Lucy said "What's that!" She opened the door to the hall. "I can hear Dad's phone ringing. Oh no!"

"What?" Steven demanded.

"His mobile's here, in his jacket pocket! Why didn't he take it?"

Steven hung up and sighed. "He changed jackets. At the last minute. He must've forgotten his mobile was in the pocket." He sat down again to think.

After a moment he stood up and told Lucy, "Well, at any rate, I can ask the workmen."

He walked over to the small caravan. He stood up on the step and knocked, then stepped down and took a pace back, to allow the door to open. When it did, a warm smell of beer, chips and cigarette smoke wafted out, and a large workman in old jeans and a grubby vest filled the doorway.

"Hello, pipsqueak! What can we do for you?" He grinned down at Steven.

"Excuse me. I was just wondering what this earth mover's for?"

"Moving earth, sunshine!" The big man roared with laughter, and his overhanging belly wobbled.

Steven didn't laugh. "Where are you going to

move earth *from*?"

"Dunno mate. We don't make the rules. Gaffer does that. We just does what we're told. Eh, Ron?"

Ron got up from the table, which was strewn with beer cans and empty chip papers. Ron was a bit older, and not such a pie-man. All muscle. Strong as an ox, Steven imagined.

"Who are you, son?" Ron asked.

"Steven MacGregor. My dad's the warden."

"Aye, well go and ask your dad, then. Said something about the top land. Told us we'd get started in the morning. Now, run along pal, and let us finish our supper."

"This, er, gaffer," Steven said quickly as the door was closing, "What did he look like?"

"Tall blond geezer – funny accent," the big man replied. "Not much like you, son. What happened?" They laughed loudly again and shut the door.

Chapter 12

On Strike

Steven went back to the cottage. Lucy was sitting at the table. She was eating a big honey sandwich, and drawing. Surprise, surprise.

Steven was in despair. He felt like crying. Mum wouldn't be back for hours. Dad was away, and couldn't even be reached on the phone. Mrs Granny was in hospital, and it looked like Jonathan Curtis was taking advantage of the situation.

And Lucy was drawing. Like she always did. As if nothing was happening.

"It *was* Jonathan Curtis who ordered the JCB," he told her. "And they *are* planning to use it on the Reach." Steven was hoping for Lucy's support, hoping for a flash of the anger that he felt, except that he was too weary and discouraged to be angry just now. But Lucy carried on chewing and drawing. Steven added, "And there's a badgers' set up there."

"Ah!" Lucy gasped with delight and looked up. "How do you know?"

"I saw it. There's cubs, too."

"When?"

"The other night."

"You never told me!"

"But they'll all be killed if the JCB goes up there. We've got to do something."

"We can't, Steve. We have to wait till Mum and Dad get back."

"Mum doesn't know why it's there, and if we wait till Dad gets back, they'll have started. We have to do something *now*!"

"Well, you know what happened last time we tried to do something."

"That was different. That was just pranks. Kids' stuff."

"Because we *are* kids!"

"Well, young people can make a difference. David the shepherd boy did. You've got to help, Lucy. Please?"

"Last time I helped, we got into awful trouble. I got a big row as well, you know. And you haven't even been to say sorry yet. He might bite your head off."

"Who?"

"Jonathan Curtis. He's big, you know. He's scary when he's angry."

"Well, so am I!" Steven stood up and clenched his fists.

Lucy laughed. "Oh yeah! I'm really frightened, Supermouse!"

"Don't be such a wimp, Lucy. Don't be such a *girl*! Are you going to help, or not?"

"I'll help when Mum and Dad get back and tell us what to do. I'm not going to help with another of your stupid ideas!"

"OK. I'll do it on my own. I don't need a *girl's* help, anyway!" He was furious. He grabbed her sketch book and held it out of reach.

"Give that back!" she demanded, making a lunge for it. "Be careful! You might tear it!"

"Be careful!" he mocked in a high voice. "You might tear it!"

"You're horrible! I hate you! You never showed me the badgers' set. You're selfish! I wish I had Graeme as a brother instead of you!" She stomped into the hall and up the stairs.

Clutching the sketch pad, Steven marched out of the cottage, and up to the JCB. He climbed up, and with a clatter, jumped down into the shovel. He sat down, breathing heavily. He didn't have a plan. He just knew he was so angry, he had to do something. He had to show everyone he was deadly serious. He was sweating, and his knees felt shaky. What now? he thought.

He didn't have long to wait. Someone hit the shovel with something heavy and metal. It sounded like thunder inside Steven's head. He put his arms up as if he'd been hit.

"Oi, sunshine! Out of there!" It was Ron's voice. "What d'you think you're doing?" His big mate was beside him. "Tony, climb up and lift him out of there."

Tony put a foot on the wheel hub. Steven jumped to his feet and looked down at them. He shouted, "Don't touch me! If you do, I'll scream blue murder! Your gaffer is *not* my father. My father's the warden of this site, and Mrs Granderton's the owner. *They* are the ones to give the orders!"

Ron and Tony were perplexed. They stepped back and muttered to each other. "Where's your dad, pal?" Tony asked. "Or your mum?"

"He's ... they're ... my mum'll be back in a few minutes." He tried to sound confident. Help! he thought. What's she going to say? What will she do?

"Come on, Tony. He'll come out when he gets tired or hungry," said Ron.

"Aye, or when he needs a pee!" They sniggered and went back to their caravan.

Steven sat down again and rested his chin on his knees. The caravan site grew quiet, and gathering clouds made darkness fall early. While he was sitting down, no-one could see him in the shovel. He shivered. He was quite cold, rather hungry and very lonely. And he didn't have any ideas. He didn't know what he was going to do. So far, everything he'd tried had failed. He wondered how David the shepherd boy would have felt. He knew that if he backed down now, he'd have lost, and everything would have been useless. Also, he'd feel very silly. He could just imagine Lucy saying, "Told you so!"

His mind wandered, and he almost dozed off, when suddenly he heard the back door of the cottage slam. He peered over the shovel, and saw Mum marching towards him.

All Steven's anger had drained away, and most of his energy had gone with it. But his determination was as strong as ever. "Hello Mum," he said quietly. "I knocked on the door of the caravan and asked the man what they were going to do with the JCB. They said their boss had told them to work on the high ground. But when I asked what the boss looked like, they described Mr Curtis. He's sneaking behind everyone's back, while Dad's away and Mrs Granny's in hospital. He's a cheat, Mum. I had to do something!"

"Well! Of all the ... But how long are you planning to stay there?"

"I don't know," Steven replied dismally.

"You've made your point, love. Why don't you come home now?"

"I can't, Mum. They'd just start digging tomorrow before Dad gets back. And Mum, I had a row with Lucy."

"I know. She told me."

There was the click of a caravan door opening, and Ron and Tony emerged out of the darkness. "Ah! Good evening Missus. This your laddie, eh?" Ron asked.

"Yes!" said Mum, standing as tall as she could, her head held high, and her eyes flashing.

"Well, he's been a brave little soldier, and now it's time to go home. Come on, pal. Tony'll help you down."

Tony reached up, but Steven repeated, "I'll scream if you lay a finger on me, and everyone on this caravan site will think you're hurting me!"

"Missus?" Tony looked at Mum.

"He's right, you know," said Mum. "There's been a mix-up. We don't want the high ground to be touched. So leave my son alone!" She took a step nearer the shovel, and stuck out her small chin.

"They're as bad as each other! Come on, Tone," said Ron. They went back to their caravan. Without a word, Mum marched over to the cottage.

"Mum!" Steven hissed after her, but she didn't turn round.

He sat down miserably. How long was he going to stay there? And how would it help, except that they couldn't use the digger with him in the shovel.

"Steven!" He peered out. Mum was back. She'd closed the door quietly and tiptoed over, so Ron and Tony wouldn't hear her. "I thought, if you're planning to stay there all night, you'd better do it in style!" She'd brought his sleeping bag, his torch, a carton of orange juice and the chips she'd promised to buy on the way back from the hospital.

"Thanks Mum!" He crawled into the sleeping bag straight away, and unwrapped the chips.

"You're your own man now, love. You're not my wee laddie any more, and I'm proud of you!"

Steven smiled through a mouthful of chips. "How's Mrs Granny?"

"I thought you'd never ask!"

"Mum!"

"Pneumonia!"

"What?"

"Pneumonia! Mrs Granny's got pneumonia!"

"That's bad, isn't it?"

"Yes, and it can kill. But in Mrs Granny's case, they've caught it in time. It could have been something worse."

"Worse? What could be worse than pneumonia?"

"Well, cancer, for a start."

"Cancer?"

"That's what *she* thought she'd got."

"But how come the doctor didn't tell her?"

"It seems she wasn't telling him the whole truth. Keeping some of the symptoms to herself. She wasn't letting on."

"Why?"

"She said that if it was her time to go, she was ready. She didn't want any operations or

chemotherapy. She's a brave lady. Very special."
Mum smiled.

Steven smiled, too. He was relieved, and he suddenly saw the funny side of it. He was peering over the shovel of a JCB in the late dark evening, talking to his mum about pneumonia!

"Did you tell her?" he asked suddenly.

"Tell her what?"

"About the ghost wolves and everything?"

"No. You can tell her when she's a bit better."

"OK."

"I'm going in now, love. Here's the back door key, just in case. Er, Steve?"

"Yep?"

"You didn't … er … do anything to Lucy's sketch pad, did you?"

"Course not, Mum. I'd forgotten about it." He tucked the key into his jeans pocket, and picked up the sketch pad from the floor of the shovel.

"Shall I take it in now for her?"

"Not till I've read it!" he said mischievously. "Good night, Mum."

He hadn't made a definite decision to stay in the shovel all night, but Mum clearly thought that's what he was planning to do. What's more, she thought he was capable of it. She was even proud of him. He felt confident again for a moment. Then he remembered the tricks he'd played on Alexander. His ideas only seemed to get him into trouble, and anyway, he'd been mean, and told lies. David had been confident God would help him, but he'd taken his sling and stones. But that had all been a long time ago. Mrs Granny's Sunday School class had seemed a long time ago, too. He'd loved all those Bible stories. He'd believed them, too. But it hadn't made any difference. He began to feel something was missing.

With a wary glance towards Ron and Tony's caravan, he snuggled down into the sleeping bag and opened the book. He began to turn the pages, and to look at the drawings in the light of his torch.

The drawings were very good. Lucy was better than he'd realised. It was a book about Scottish wildlife: animals, birds, insects, trees and plants. Beside each drawing was some information, copied out in Lucy's beautiful handwriting. He knew some of the facts, but not all.

"Red squirrels," he read, "spend most of their time feeding on pine kernels. Many Scots pines in the forest are very old. Over the years, many natural pines have been felled. The two World Wars used up large areas of Caledonian Pine Forest, where pines mingle with birch, rowan and juniper."

Lucy had drawn examples of each of these trees, as well as a red squirrel nibbling pine kernels.

"Scientists interested in conserving wildlife have created new plantations of pines, to replace some of those which were felled," he read on. He turned the pages. There was a drawing of a bat, and of the 'Tanglewood Wedge', a bat box where bats sleep safely upside down, protected from predators. There were lots of drawings of moths and butterflies, and of the sort of plants each type needed. Steven was absorbed. Perhaps Lucy will become a scientist, he thought. Maybe a biologist. He turned page after page, admiring the careful, detailed drawings and soaking up the information.

After a while, he began to feel uncomfortable. He shifted his position. He became even more uncomfortable, and realised it was because he needed the toilet.

Crumbs! Tony was right! He knew he couldn't get out of the shovel and back in again silently, and he couldn't risk waking them up. He knew that if they found he'd got out, they'd stop him getting back in again. Jonathan Curtis would have won.

He had an idea. He stood up and cupped his hands as if to catch a butterfly. Then he put his mouth over his thumb knuckles and blew gently. Years ago, he and Lucy had learnt to make a tawny owl call. He tried it now, facing towards the cottage.

'Whoo, whoo,' he blew. He waited, then tried again.

Sure enough, he saw Lucy's bedroom curtains twitch. Her face appeared at the window. He waved and beckoned. She waved back, then disappeared. He wondered if she'd gone back to bed. Just for a moment, his determination wavered. It would feel so good to let himself in the back door, go to the toilet, then get into his own bed. He couldn't remember what he'd thought was funny when he leaned out talking to Mum. Lucy had said he was stupid. She was probably right. Whatever was he doing in a shovel, in the middle of the night, needing the toilet, and with no proper plans? The situation was desperate, and he couldn't see any way out of it.

To his amazement, his own bedroom window opened. Lucy climbed out and down the drainpipe, dropping nimbly to the ground. She ran noiselessly over to the shovel.

"Hi!" she whispered.

"Hi."

"Steve, I ..."

"Sorry Lucy," he said at the same time.

"I don't think you're stupid. I think you're brave."

"And you're not a wimp. You're better than most boys, any day!"

She smiled. "Are you OK?"

"Yes, but I need the loo!"

"Mum said she'd given you a key."

"Yes, but if they ..." he nodded towards Ron and Tony's caravan, "If they see I've got out, they'll block my way. Not let me back in again. And I'll have lost."

"Oh!"

"So will *you* get in here while I go?"

"OK. But what if ..."

"If they come near, tell them not to touch you, or you'll scream!"

"OK." She grinned. Steven felt confident about Lucy's yelling.

So they swapped places for a couple of minutes. When Steven came back, Lucy asked, "How long are you going to stay there?"

"I don't know, but at any rate I could stop them using the shovel. Even if I have to stay in here until Dad gets back ... Anyway, how did you learn to climb out of my bedroom window?"

"Easy!" she said airily. "I'm going to climb back in now!" And off she went.

He was on his own in the silence. He looked up

at a million bright stars, and whispered, "Lord God, what am I going to do? I can't do it without you, Lord. I just make a mess of things. But I want to be like David, who trusted you. Not like one of the soldiers who did nothing."

The stars seemed so near, he felt he could reach out and touch them, and he didn't feel alone at all. He lay down and dozed. Around dawn, a light drizzle began to fall. The stars were hidden by clouds. Steven woke up shivering, and pulled the sleeping bag over his head. He pushed Lucy's book to the bottom of the bag and fell into a deep sleep.

Chapter 13

A New Day

When Steven woke up, it was fully light. A thick mist clung to the hillside, but there was no fog in his mind. Suddenly it was clear to him what he should do. He thought of David standing in front of Goliath, fearless, determined, and certain that God was going to help him.

Stretching, and flexing his stiff, cold muscles, Steven peered over the shovel. Four or five small children were standing around the JCB. They were amazed to see his head appear, and they ran off in all directions. Steven sat down and took a few deep breaths.

Soon, the little children reappeared, and before long, it seemed every child on the site was there. Someone started to chant his name low and rhythmically: Ste-ven, Ste-ven! Listening to it, Steven was encouraged. They were mostly his friends, out there. The chanting fed his determination, and gave him as much energy as a good square meal. Soon, it became a clapped rhythm: clap clap, clap clap clap, clap clap clap clap, STEVEN! They repeated it, louder and louder, faster and faster, till his name filled the whole caravan site.

Steven had often wondered what pole vaulters and triple jumpers thought about in those moments before their run-up. Now he knew! He breathed slowly and calmly. Adrenalin rushed around his body. His mind was focussed. The chanting changed to cheering, and Steven stood up, tall and straight, in the middle of the shovel. He looked round, slowly and confidently. Tony and Ron were leaning against their caravan. Mum and Lucy were outside the back door of the cottage. He could see Graeme and his mum and dad beside their caravan. There were many more, adults and children, people he knew, and people he didn't. The cheering stopped and everyone was looking at Steven. Their faces were open and hopeful. They wondered what was going to happen next.

"Hi everyone!" said Steven, as loudly, clearly and calmly as he could. "You're probably wondering what I'm doing in here, in fact, why I've spent the whole night in here." He spoke slowly, giving everyone a chance to realise. A ripple of amazement went round the crowd. "It's because I wanted to do something, *anything*, to stop the top of Mrs Granderton's land being over-developed. Many of you will have read our fliers about the threat to the site. Some of you have signed our petition to say you agree with us. Thank you. Let me explain what we're on about." There was a general shuffling and murmuring, as people got ready to listen.

"For years, the people who own and run this site have tried to make it a friendly place, not just for people, but for animals, birds and plants, as well. We try to keep it safe, clean and litter-free, so it's hygienic and looks nice." He looked around again. There wasn't a sound. Everyone was listening carefully. He couldn't see Mr Robertson any longer, but Graeme and Mrs Robertson had moved down to stand a bit nearer.

"Rubbish areas are hidden behind bushes so they don't look a mess. There are skips ..." he pointed, "... for recycling paper, glass bottles, tin cans, aluminium cans and plastic. Please use them whenever you can." There was a general murmur of agreement.

"If a lot more people stayed on the site, what we've got wouldn't be enough, and the place would begin to look a mess. Some people would like to have more entertainments on the site, like a club house or a café. We've got some good friends in the village who run a café and a club, and they'd be very happy to have some more customers." He grinned, and people chuckled.

Steven looked around again, and noticed Jonathan Curtis and Alexander standing on the bank outside Mrs Granny's garden. He gathered all his courage and continued, "But the most important question is whether the land at the top of the site is dug up, *by this earth-mover*, to put more caravans there. If we did that, I'll tell you what would happen. Lots of trees would have to be cut down first. The woodland up there is part of the Great Caledonian Pine Forest. It's mainly made up of Scots pines. Red squirrels eat pine kernels. Red squirrels are already in danger from grey squirrels, 'cos grey ones are bigger. If we take away some of their food and habitat, they'll be in even more danger. Loads of trees were cut down in the First and Second World Wars, for making equipment. Isn't it up to us to make sure no more get cut down?" He could see heads nodding, and hear murmurs of agreement.

"Already some Scottish animals have become extinct, like wolves and lynx and elk. If we're not careful, we won't have any more wildcats or even badgers." Steven's mind was like a computer memory, and Lucy's book was printed on it.

"Do you know how many species of moth can be found in Scotland?" He looked round, like a teacher. Lucy was grinning and nodding. "Four hundred and ninety-seven," he told them. "They need very particular things to survive, like special plants, and tree bark to camouflage their chrysalises." Steven noticed that Alexander was standing a bit closer now, and that Mrs Curtis had joined her husband on the bank.

"We're probably not sorry that there are no wolves in Scotland any longer. But lots of people would be sorry ... I know I would." He looked towards Alexander. Their eyes locked. "*Very sorry*, if we lost wildcats, or butterflies, or golden eagles, or ... or ... or anything which is part of our Scottish environment." He'd looked at Alexander without blinking through the whole of his last sentence. He couldn't be sure, but he thought Alexander nodded slightly. Steven stopped and swallowed.

"But what's more," he continued, "that top land belongs to Mrs Granderton herself. The whole site does." He wondered how many people knew Mrs Granny personally. "She's always loved the top bit particularly. It's got lots of trees and plants and wildlife. And lovely views. Up to now she has never wanted to put caravans up there. She says we should let the land breathe. She's not very well just now, and she's in hospital ..." People gasped with surprise and concern.

"Digging work is supposed to start this morning. My father, the warden, is away doing a job for Mrs Granderton today, and he's not due back till this evening. But I don't think ..." At this point Steven's heart began to thump, and a tell-tale lump sprang to his throat. He swallowed hard and repeated, "But I don't think any work should be started before we're absolutely sure that's what Mrs Granderton wants. And I hope you'll all agree with me."

Steven ran out of words. He was suddenly exhausted and terribly thirsty. It took him a few seconds to realise that the whole crowd, almost a hundred adults and children, were cheering and clapping and jumping up and down. Mum and Lucy were beaming and dancing a jig. Tony and Ron were grinning. There was no sign of Mr Curtis, but Alexander and his mother were standing next to Graeme and Mrs Robertson. Mrs Curtis looked unusually serious.

Mr Robertson came marching through the crowd and stood next to the shovel. "Well done, Steven," he said quietly. "What a pity your dad missed that!" After a minute or two more, he held up his hand, and everyone grew quiet.

"Ladies and gentlemen of the jury!" he began in a loud, clear, public voice. There was a chuckle from the people who knew he was a lawyer. "I think we'd all like to say well done to Steven MacGregor, for putting us in the picture." More cheers and claps. "And I, for one, agree with him wholeheartedly!" More cheers.

"But the time has come for us to look at the legal side of all this. Mrs Granderton's solicitor, Neville McAllister, has been a friend of mine since law school. When my son Graeme, Steven's pal, told me of some of the problems Steven has been speaking about, I took the liberty of going to see Neville, and asking where we stood on this one. I was interested to hear that Mrs Granderton revised her will recently, just the other day, in fact, immediately after revisiting Hooper's Reach. We hear she's on the mend, and we hope her will won't have to be read for a long while yet. But Neville told me Mrs Granderton had said that *on no account ...*" Mr Robertson stood to attention, and Steven thought he looked every inch a lawyer, despite his jeans and T-shirt, "*... on no account* should the top ground be developed for caravans. Now, if that's what Mrs Granderton wanted after she died, then of course that land should remain unspoilt during her lifetime. So, gentlemen," he turned to Ron and Tony, "I'm afraid we won't be needing your services."

Tony and Ron looked at each other, shrugged their shoulders, and went inside their caravan.

Mr Robertson held up his arms for Steven to jump down, and a final cheer went up from the crowd. Before jumping, Steven dropped the precious sketch book into Lucy's waiting hands. "Cool book, sis," he told her.

Inside the cottage, Mum hugged Steven tightly. She couldn't stop grinning. "How about a bowl of cereal, a hot shower and a sleep?" she offered.

"Yeah!" Steven breathed with his last ounce of

energy. "Drink first, please."

"What about the Holiday Club?" Lucy demanded.

"I think he needs to give it a miss today," Mum said.

"OK," Lucy agreed.

"Say sorry to Amanda for me," Steven said.

"Amanda, eh?" Lucy grinned.

Steven took a swipe at her, but she dodged into the hall, and he missed.

"When Dad gets back we'll go and visit Mrs Granny," Mum said quickly before Lucy disappeared upstairs to get ready. "I phoned the hospital. She's definitely on the way up."

Lucy called "OK," then stuck her head round the door to add, "Cool speech, bro!"

Chapter 14

A New Start

It took a long time to fill Dad in when he returned from Inverness. Steven told the story modestly, but Lucy and Mum kept chipping in to say how brave and brilliant he'd been.

"You should've heard the cheering and clapping, Dad!" Lucy said. "It was better than 'Top of the Pops!'"

"Never mind the cheering, you should've heard the speech, love!" Mum insisted. "You'd have been very proud of our lad! And our lass, too. She certainly played her part!"

"I'm very proud of all of you," Dad assured them. I'm really sorry I didn't hear it first hand. But …"

"But what?" the three of them chorused.

"But I need to have a word with Jonathan Curtis in the morning. He's getting a bit big for his boots! He'd no business to make those arrangements behind my back – and Rhoda's."

Mum, Dad and Lucy were still talking about it when they reached the hospital. Steven was thinking. He wanted to tell Mrs Granny that God had helped him. He knew she'd understand. She had belonged to God since she was a girl. But he wasn't sure how to start.

"Just go easy on Mrs Granny," Mum warned Steven and Lucy as they got out of the van at the hospital. "She's been very poorly, and she's still pretty weak."

Steven and Lucy suddenly felt awkward as they were shown to Mrs Granny's bed. "There *should* be only two visitors at a time," the nurse scolded, "But since you're family ..."

"Well, actually ...." Dad began.

"I know. She told me. Clan MacGregor, she said." The nurse grinned as if they were all sharing a secret, and Steven felt so proud he thought he would burst.

"But what about ..." Lucy whispered to Mum.

"Now, if she seems to be getting tired ...." the nurse continued.

"We know, nurse. We won't stay too long," Dad reassured her.

Mrs Granny was overjoyed to see them. After hugs all round, Lucy sat next to her and held her thin hand. Mum asked her how she was, and Dad told her he'd had a successful trip to Inverness.

Steven felt tongue-tied. He didn't know how to say just a little, since such a lot had happened. Finally, Mrs Granny asked, "How was the Holiday Club?"

"Great! I enjoyed it. I might start going to STEP."

"You'll enjoy that, too. They're a great bunch of youngsters, and I know they have a lot of fun."

"Especially if Amanda's there!" Lucy put in, grinning mischievously at Steven.

But Mrs Granny continued, "I gather you've got lots more to tell me, Steven, but you'll come and see me again tomorrow?"

"Yeah!" said Steven, laughing. Trust Mrs Granny to make it easy for him.

"And if you *can* come tomorrow, could you do something for me?"

"Sure!"

"If I'm going to stick around on this earth a bit longer after all, there are some letters I need to answer. They're in a bundle with a rubber band round, on my coffee table. Could you bring them in for me tomorrow, dear?"

"Yep. No problem. Oh … Mrs Granny?"

"Yes, dear?"

"Who was Hooper? You know, Hooper's Reach."

"Well, no-one's really sure, but the story in the village is an old romantic one. Several centuries ago there was an Irishman called Seamus Hooper, who sailed his boat over here every month to visit his sweetheart who lived in the village. She used to light two fires, one at the highest point of the land, before the forest started, the other half-way down, probably about where the Robertsons' caravan is, to guide him to the shore. When he had both fires lined up in his sights, he knew he could sail a safe passage between the rocks. In a village, everyone knows everyone else's business, so the whole village was keen to see Hooper land his boat safely. Eventually they married and she went off to Ireland with him."

"Ah! How sweet!" Lucy purred.

"So Hooper wasn't Scottish at all. He was an Irishman?" Steven checked.

"That's how the story goes, dear!"

"And Hooper never owned the land?"

"Not so far as we know. Why?"

"Oh, I just wondered."

When they arrived home, Steven ran along to Mrs Granny's house straight away, before going into the cottage. He wanted to fetch the letters, and say sorry to Mr Curtis. Somehow, like David standing in front of King Saul, he didn't feel afraid any more.

There was no reply when he rang the doorbell, so he went round to the back and knocked. Still no reply. He tried the door. It wasn't locked. Slowly, he ventured inside and called, "Hello?" The house was silent. He peered into the kitchen and dining-room, and then the sitting-room. The letters were there. He picked them up. Then he crept upstairs. He called "Hello! Anyone in?" before going into the bedrooms. Mrs Granny's bed was neatly made, ready for her return. He peeped into the two spare rooms, where Alexander and his parents had been sleeping. The bedclothes were folded tidily at the end of each bed, and there was no sign of any suitcases or personal possessions.

"They've gone!" Steven said aloud, in amazement. He stood, puzzled. Then he had an idea. He ran down and opened the cupboard under the stairs. The wooden toolbox was gone, but on the floor where it used to stand, was a small screwed-up note. Steven unfolded it and recognised Mrs Granny's handwriting. It read 'For my cousin, Alexander Curtis'.

Steven's idea grew. He rushed into the sitting-room. The sword, shield and tartan were still on the wall, and a small piece of paper was taped to the shield. Steven read, 'For my distant relative Steven, a true MacGregor.'

Steven felt warm and happy. He smiled round the

empty living room, and he told the shield, "She was getting ready to die, but she didn't forget me." He would enjoy owning the shield and sword one day, but not for a long time. For now, he was very pleased to have Mrs Granny. He left the paper as if he'd never seen it, and took a last look around the room. There was a letter propped up behind the clock on the mantelpiece. Steven picked it up. It was addressed to 'Rhoda' and it was sealed. He put it back thoughtfully, then ran home.

"Dad! Dad!" Steven tore through the kitchen and into the hall.

Dad's voice came from upstairs. "How'd it go, son?"

"Dad, they've gone! Suitcases. Everything." As he spoke, he noticed a piece of paper had been pushed through the letter box. He picked it up. It had his name on it. He unfolded it and read,

'Steven, it's all right about the ghost wolves. You don't need to say sorry. I think you are right. I'm sure my dad will agree in the end. I think we should all let the land breathe. A.'

"Well!" Mum exclaimed, reading over Steven's shoulder.

"So they're really gone, then," Dad murmured, coming down the stairs. "I guess that solves a few problems. I used to doubt the family tree story, but apparently it's true. Rhoda's lawyer checked. It's just that they were so different from her …"

"Anne-Marie was OK," Mum objected. "Really friendly. Seemed like she wanted to settle."

"Well I'm glad they've gone," Lucy said. "Now we don't have to share Mrs Granny any more."

But Steven was sorry, somehow. He had hoped to

show Alexander how to use the tools. They could have made bird boxes, and extended the hide. If Hooper's Reach stayed free, they could have watched badgers together. He wanted to take Alexander to the Holiday Club. Perhaps he'd have gone to STEP, too ...

If you've enjoyed this book why not look out for...

The Tunnel Seekers
Anne Thorne

When Beth, who is an only child, goes to stay with her cousins, they enjoy an action-packed summer. Beth discovers how to be more confident. But their adventure in the tunnel also shows them the danger of acting without thinking first.

ISBN 1 85999 226 9

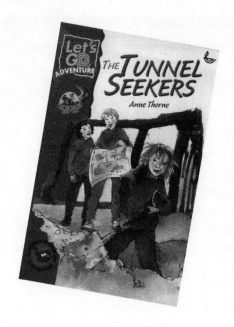

Flood Alert!
Kathy Lee

It was stupid, I know that now. But there was no time to think. Helpless as a bit of straw, I was tossed and shaken and dragged under water. I fought my way up – then before I could snatch a breath I went under again.

"Help!" I shouted.

"Don't bother," said Kerry. "They won't hear."

I was sinking. I was going down for the last time...

An exciting story of two young friends whose lives are threatened when a period of atrocious weather leads to flooding in their village. The book also covers the themes of being a Christian at school and friendship with non-Christians. A Snapshots title.

ISBN 1 85999 301 X

Lion Hunt
Ruth Kirtley

High time, short point at four.
Climb a lofty guardian;
What stops his roar?

The clues seem baffling. Will Ashley and
Rachel be able to work
them out in time? And
will the clues lead them
to something that will
save the house from
being taken over by the
scheming Mr Doubleby?

For Ashley, too, there is
much more to this than a
hunt for hidden loot. A
Snapshots title.

ISBN 1 85999 412 1

*You can buy these books at your local Christian
bookshop, or online at
www.scriptureunion.org.uk/publishing
or call Mail Order direct
01908 856006*